About the A

Denis Bond has written over seventy many picture books for younger readers, such as *The Train Who Was Frightened Of The Dark* and *The Brave Sea Captain*. His books for older readers include *Avenue* and *It's A Boy Girl Thing* while his teen-romances, written under the name of Denise Colby, feature the titles *Love Dreams* and *Will You Still Love Me Tomorrow?* He has also written for children's TV and radio, working on a string of successful programmes including *Rainbow*, *Pipkins*, *The Munch Bunch*, *The Listening Corner*, *Let's Pretend* and *Picme*. Having originally trained for the theatre, he worked as an actor before spending some years as a teacher. He now combines all three skills in his action-packed author visits and writers' workshops in schools and libraries throughout the UK and abroad.

His website is www.denisbond.co.uk

POP RIVALS

Denis Bond

Matador
9 Priory Business Park
Kibworth Beauchamp
Leicestershire LE8 0RX, UK
Tel: (+44) 116 279 2299
Fax: (+44) 116 279 2277
Email: books@troubador.co.uk
Web: www.troubador.co.uk/matador

ISBN 978 1780885 698

British Library Cataloguing in Publication Data.
A catalogue record for this book is available from the British Library.

Printed and bound in the UK by TJ International, Padstow, Cornwall
Typeset in Palatino by Troubador Publishing Ltd

Matador is an imprint of Troubador Publishing Ltd

For Ken

One

The light from the police car flashed on and off, lighting the trailer's small bedroom: blue-black, blue-black, blue-black.

Terry Smith leapt out of bed and reached across to his brother, gently shaking him awake.

"Billy. It's the gavvers." He slipped on his jeans and grabbed for his tattered trainers.

Billy moaned. "What do they want this time?"

Terry reached for his glasses and crossed into the passage which separated their room from their parents' bedroom. His mother was sitting on the edge of her double bed, staring into space.

"Where's Dad?" he asked.

"Out there. I tried to stop him, but you know what he's like. Always has to get involved."

Billy joined them. "What do they want?"

Mother shrugged. "I think they're at Mick Mahoney's trailer."

Terry returned to his room and put on his sweater.

"Don't you get mixed up in it, Terry," his mother called.

"If Dad's out there, we should *all* be!" he replied.

He leapt down the trailer's steps just as the shouting began.

Mick Mahoney was yelling from his trailer window. "What d'yer want from me this time?"

One police officer called out to him, "Just a word, Mick. Get dressed and come and have a chat, eh?"

Mick Mahoney responded aggressively, "I remember the last chat we had, when you bruised me ribs, yer bunch o' little 'itlers!"

The police officer neared the trailer. "If you don't come out, we'll come and get you."

Terry's father approached the officer. "What's he supposed to have done?"

Another officer, younger, took his arm. "Why don't you go back to your caravan, Josh? This one's got nothing to do with you... for a change."

Joshua Smith pulled his arm away. "If you're arresting one of ours, it's got everything to do with *all* of us, yer gorja pigs!"

Levi yelled as he crossed the mud from *his* trailer. "He's been with us all night, in the pub. So he can't have done nuffink."

A second police car, light flashing, siren wailing, entered the campsite.

Josh began to rage. "*Two* paddy-wagons?" What you expectin'? A riot or suvink?"

Four officers leapt from the second car.

Terry came to his father's side. "Leave it, Dad. Please. You know what Mick Mahoney's like."

Josh turned on his son. "Get back to bed. This ain't nuffink to do with yous."

Billy joined them. "He's probably been nicking from the estate, Dad."

"He's been with us all night!" snapped Josh. "He ain't nicked nuffink. But that won't stop em locking him up, will it? Look what they done to *me*."

"It ain't nicking from the estate we're worried about this time, Josh," said the younger officer. "It's a bit more serious than that."

"He's been with us all night," argued Levi. "In The Three Stars. Then a takeaway."

"What sort of takeaway?" asked the police officer, with a sneer.

Mick Mahoney left the trailer window.

The officer called back over his shoulder, "He's coming out!"

The trailer door burst open and a scrawny, snarling Alsatian, lips curled back, leapt down the steps and sank his teeth into the young officer's thigh.

Mick Mahoney screamed out, "Get him!"

Two officers rushed to their colleague's aid and tried to pull the dog off. It turned, snapping at both of them, before taking a second bite at the bloodied leg. A baton was raised and the Alsatian was beaten about the head until it fell unconscious in the mud.

"My dog!" shouted Mick Mahoney.

Josh grabbed the younger officer around the neck and dragged him to the ground.

"Dad! Don't!" yelled Terry. He and Billy backed away to their trailer's steps, where their mother stood, pathetically eyeing the scene.

"I knew it," she said, softly. "He'll be sent down again. I knew it."

As one officer radioed for help – "Assistance urgently required at the Berryfield gypsy camp…" – travellers and police lashed out at each other, tumbling over in the mud, punching and beating each other with sticks and batons. All the dogs were unleashed, adding to the mayhem, barking, growling and snapping at everyone, whether gypsy or gorja.

"Get inside, you twos," said Terry's mother.

Billy yelled, "Dad! Come away!"

Josh had given the young gavver a good belting and left him groaning in the mud. He turned to look back at his trailer, yelling, "Get to bed, will yous? Leave it to us!"

As the blue lights, still flashing on and off, lit up Josh's face, Terry thought he looked strange. Pained. He'd seen his father in fights before. Many times. But tonight was different. Josh enjoyed a good fight and always emerged, even with a bruised cheek or a split lip, like the conquering hero, grinning and bright-eyed. But tonight he looked sickly.

Mother knew immediately that something was wrong and rushed down the steps towards him. "Josh?"

He was wheezing, trying to catch his breath. "Get me indoors."

She took his arm and led him towards the trailer. Billy rushed to help, taking the other arm.

Terry stood at the foot of the trailer steps, staring, unable to move.

Josh, supported by his wife and younger son, managed to climb slowly to the top step, where he clutched the door frame, gasping, one fist pressed against his chest.

"You're all right, Dad," said Billy, trying desperately to reassure his father and himself. "You're okay."

Josh lost his grip on the door frame and was too weak to grab for it again. He tumbled backwards down the steps, landing at Terry's feet.

His wife screamed out, desperately, "Call an ambulance!"

No-one heard her cries above the shouting and beating and barking.

She turned to Terry. "Quick! Ask Jane to use the phone!"

Terry didn't move.

"Terry!"

Billy saw that his brother *couldn't* move.

"I'll go, Mum!" he shouted as he sped across the campsite.

Terry watched him disappearing, until the stiffness left his limbs… and then he ran, overtaking Billy and heading for the main house.

Two

Terry was pleased with the first verse. He sang it to himself over and over again. He just hoped that it was original, that he wasn't copying something he'd heard on the radio. He sang it again, louder this time as there was no-one to hear him. The rest of them would have reached the river by now. Terry was always last. Who cared? He hated cross-country running. He hated Jamieson even more. And what good did cross-country running do anyway?

"It gets those lungs working properly, lads!" yelled Mr Jamieson.

Terry's lungs were all right as they were. The voice proved it!

> "Call on me
> When you are lonely
> Though I know I can only
> Be a friend..."

He was going to be a star. No doubt about it! Though he knew it wouldn't come easy. Not with his background. Not like it would for some. But if determination to succeed meant anything at all, then nothing would stop him from going all the way to the top.

Jamieson turned back from the park gates and cut through the wood to the gravel path, along which most of his year eleven boys had run. Three were missing. He knew who they were and was irritated that his least favourite was among them. Smith. Terry Smith.

Terry shuffled along the path, running in short spurts, walking then running again. His feet hurt. His bright red tee shirt only helped to show how pale his arms were. Pale and thin. His shorts, supposedly white, but leaning towards grey, were *too* short. He daydreamed of appearing on one of those pop TV programmes where unknown singers competed against each other: pop stars created from nobodies with undiscovered talent. He definitely had the talent. If only he could get onto a show like that and prove to the world that he was a superstar in the making.

"If you knew
How much it hurts me
To be left on the outside,
Looking in..."

Bob Jamieson stepped out from the wood onto the path. He could see the boy approaching in the distance, the sun glinting of his spectacles. Terry stopped, placing a hand over his forehead and squinting.

Jamieson bellowed, "Get a move on, Smith! You're not out for a Sunday stroll!"

Terry quickened his pace, despite the pain in his heels.

"Move it, lad! You're puffing like my old granny!"

He limped the last few yards and stopped in the teacher's shadow.

"What's the matter with you?" sneered Jamieson.

"It's my feet."

"Sir!"

"It's my feet... *sir!*"

Jamieson looked down at the tattered trainers. "It's no wonder is it, lad? Look at the state of those."

"They're my brother's... *sir!*"

"Your brother's?"

"Yes."

"He's only in year nine! No wonder they don't fit!"

Terry looked away, avoiding the icy-blue stare. He was afraid of the powerfully-built teacher. He feared him and he envied him. He coveted his body and the long, blond hair which flopped over his ruggedly handsome face. He envied him and he hated him.

"Where's *yours*?"

"I need some new ones. I'm getting some as soon as Dad comes home."

Jamieson longed to ask, "Home from where, Smith?"

Terry's eyes began to well up. "My dad's in hospital," he said. He whipped off his glasses, their thin frame catching the tiny piece of sticky-plaster which covered his earring; a school rule when doing sports.

"Is he? I'm sorry to hear that, Smith."

"He is!" Terry suddenly shouted. "I know you don't believe me!"

Jamieson was shocked at the sudden aggression. "Who said I don't believe you?"

"He's in hospital with his heart!" Terry's whole body was beginning to shake. He whipped off his glasses, which were steaming up. "He's not in prison, this time! He's in hospital!"

He turned and sped back along the gravel path, forgetting the pain in his feet.

Jamieson bawled after him, "Come back here, Smith!"

Terry didn't hear him. He could hear nothing but the pounding of his heart and his heavy breathing as he ran faster and faster towards the disused drinking fountain. He leapt a low fence, crossed the putting green and ran on into the rhododendrons, where he collapsed on the ground and sobbed.

"What's that noise?" whispered Scotty. He placed a hand on Rosetti's arm. Listen."

Ray Rosetti took the cigarette from his lips and cocked his head on one side.

Scotty whispered again, "This way."

They trod lightly through the rhododendrons, following the sound which changed from a sob to a low whimper. Terry heard them approach. He hurriedly wiped his eyes on the back of his hand and replaced his glasses.

"Well, if it isn't Smithy!" grinned Phillip Scott. "What are *you* doing here?"

Terry scrambled to his feet. "I didn't know anyone was here."

"Well you do now!" snarled Rosetti.

"He's all right," said Scotty. "He won't say nothing." He

produced a cigarette packet from his shorts' pocket, opened it and offered it to Terry. "Here, d'you wanna fag, Smithy?"

"I don't smoke," replied Terry.

Ray Rosetti mimicked the boy's voice. "I don't smoke." He took a long drag on his cigarette and held the smoke for a few seconds before letting it out in a series of rings.

Scotty watched, admiringly.

"What *do* you do, Smith?" asked Rosetti. "Apart from stink?"

Terry turned and began to walk away.

Rosetti called after him. "Oi! Pikey! Where do you think you're going?"

Terry stopped in his tracks, turned back and glared.

Rosetti approached him, menacingly. "I don't think we said he could go, did we, Scotty?"

Scotty followed his mate.

"Come here, Smith!" added Rosetti.

Terry didn't move.

Rosetti held out his half-smoked cigarette towards the boy. "Here. Have a drag."

"No."

"You're not going to grass us up, are you, Smith?" asked Scotty.

"*I* don't care what you do," Terry replied.

Ray Rosetti took a final drag on his cigarette, threw the stub at his feet and worked it into the ground with the toe of his trainer. "Do you think we can trust him, Scotty?" he asked as he calmly removed Terry's glasses with one hand and held them in the air. "I suppose you could always say that you didn't see us, can't you, Smithy?"

"Give me them. Please," pleaded Terry.

"Oh, come on, Ray," said Scotty. "Give them to him."

Scotty had begun to feel sorry for the boy, as he often did. He knew there was the choice, of course: either run with the hounds or be chased by them. From day one, Scotty had decided to join Rosetti's pack.

"These ain't half strong, Smithy," smirked Rosetti, as he placed the glasses on the end of his nose. "You must be nearly blind."

"Give them to me, please," said Terry. "I can't see."

Rosetti retreated further into the rhododendrons. "Aaah, can't you see, Smithy?" he called. "Then you won't be able to see where I'm burying them, will you?" He fell to his knees and covered the glasses with a pile of twigs.

Scotty decided he'd had enough. "I'm going back, Ray," he said. "Give us me matches!"

Rosetti took the matches from his shorts' pocket and handed them to Scotty, who hurried off towards the putting green.

"I'll see you later!" he called.

"Hold on!" Rosetti called after him. "I'm coming!" He placed his hands on Terry's shoulders and began to spin him round. "Bit like blind man's buff, isn't it?"

Terry hit out at Rosetti, but missed. Rosetti was surprised. He was angry, yet amused. People didn't hit him. Ever!

"Here, what's this?" he said threateningly. "You didn't try to punch me, did you, Smith?"

"Give me my glasses!"

"Because people who punch me, especially filthy, little gyppos, get punched back, right?" He held his clenched fist in front of Terry's face, as a warning. Then he decided he might as well use it. After all, he hadn't hit anyone for weeks.

He punched Terry in the mouth.

Terry yelped and put a hand to his split lip.

"Don't be late for the shower, will you, Smith?" laughed Rosetti as he strolled after Scotty across the putting green.

Three

Bob Jamieson, lounging on a chair in the centre of the hall, watched as Ray Rosetti set up his band's equipment on the school stage.

Jim Buckley, Head of English, pulled up a second chair and sat beside the PE teacher. "As if I haven't got anything better to do," he moaned.

Jamieson laughed. "They might be good. You never know, you may be witnessing the birth of a future pop supergroup."

Jim Buckley smiled. "I doubt it."

Rosetti carefully began to manoeuvre an amplifier into its correct position as his girlfriend, the beautiful blonde-haired Maureen, looked on, admiringly.

Jim Buckley smiled again. "What on Earth does she see in Ray Rosetti? She's such a nice girl."

Jamieson shrugged. "He's a handsome guy, that's why."

The other members of the band, having set everything up, joined their lead singer and his girlfriend on stage and began to tune up their instruments. The Leroy twins, John and Mark, similarly gauche in appearance, toothpick thin and with blond (almost white) hair atop their pimpled faces, picked up their guitars as one and strummed.

Jamieson stifled a laugh. "I didn't know *they* were in Rosetti's band. That'll put the girls off."

Jim Buckley laughed out loud. "From what I hear, *they're* the talent!"

Scotty suddenly started pounding away on the drums, making Jamieson jump. "I'm really looking forward to this," he said, sarcastically. "All my favourite pupils in one group."

"And talking of your favourites," said Jim Buckley, raising his voice above the tuning guitars, "what happened to Terry Smith today?"

"I've no idea," replied Jamieson. "Why? What d'you mean?"

"He came in from the run, fifteen minutes late... with a cut lip."

"Oh yeah. I saw that." He laughed. "I didn't do it."

"Didn't you ask him who *did*?"

Jamieson sighed. "What's the point? Every word that kid utters is a lie. Anyway, you're his form teacher. You ask him."

Jim Buckley defended the boy as usual. "He doesn't lie."

Jamieson raised his eyebrows. "Like his dad being in hospital, you mean?"

"Is that what he said?" Jim was surprised.

Bob Jamieson sneered. "Hospital! Yeah, right!"

"Perhaps it's true."

Bob laughed. "The last time his dad was in prison, he told you he was in Australia, didn't he?"

"Yes."

"Visiting relatives."

"That's what he said."

Bob grinned. "I'm sure Sydney's full of pikeys."

"It's a shame," said Jim. "He's very bright, you know. The only one of mine who'll leave here with any decent qualifications."

"That *is* a shame," replied Bob. "He's the only one who won't *need* qualifications. He'll get by the same way as his father does."

"We're nearly ready, sir!" Maureen called.

"I'm sorry, Jim," said Jamieson. "I know he's one of your favourites."

Jim Buckley stared ahead at the stage. "I just feel sorry for him, that's all. Don't forget I've got those two good-for-nothing yobbos in the same form." He nodded towards Rosetti and Scotty. "Totally useless and spoiled to death. They make Terry Smith seem like an angel."

"At least you've got Maureen to brighten your day," replied Jamieson. "You haven't got to put up with those twins: The Personality Brothers. The Leroys! The Pimply Duo!"

Jim laughed. "Perhaps they should call their band The Zits!"

Both teachers guffawed loudly, catching Rosetti's attention.

"We're ready, sir!" he called.

"Okay, Ray!" Jim called back. "Let's be hearing you."

"What *do* they call themselves?" whispered Jamieson.
Jim smiled. "Bury The Rabbit!"
Jamieson's jaw dropped. "Bury The *what*?"

Maureen had been going out with Rosetti for six months, since she'd joined his band. He was the first real boyfriend she'd had, though she'd never been short of offers. She'd always been popular with the boys and not just because of her good looks. She also had a great sense of humour. Those girls who weren't jealous of her often remarked what a good-looking couple she and Ray Rosetti made, her delicate features and short, blonde hair helping him to appear darker, tougher and more handsome than he already was.

Occasionally one of the older boys, unaware of her steady relationship, would ask her out. She would always refuse, though she was careful not to offend. She was content to be with Rosetti. He could afford the lifestyle she enjoyed. He had two rooms to himself at the top of his parents' house, a top of the range computer, a TV and the best cut clothes of anyone his age. He also had enough money to take her out every Saturday night.

"This one's called 'EASY!'" Rosetti announced into the microphone. He turned to the rest of his band: "A-one, a-two, a-one, two, three, four...!"
Scotty and the Leroys blasted a deafening sound from the stage.
"Here we go," grinned Jamieson.

Rosetti sang:

"Didn't take to schoolin'; got no int'rest
Couldn't take to doin' what I had to do.
I'm rebellin' to prove I'm somethin',
I aim to get me somewhere... telling you!"

Maureen joined him, singing:

"And it's easy!
You know what I mean?
Easy!"

Jamieson turned to Jim Buckley. "They're a bit loud!"

Rosetti's voice was harsh, and the less-amplified Maureen could hardly be heard. Jim wondered how he would tell them, in the kindest possible way, that their voices didn't really blend. They'd approached him earlier in the week and asked if they could play at the school dance but Jim had said that he'd have to listen to them first.

"My dad'll bring everything in the van," said Rosetti. "He reckons we're really good and he's going to manage us."

"Really?"

Franco Rosetti had given his son everything that money could buy and Jim wasn't surprised to hear that he was also prepared to put cash into Ray's dream of becoming a pop star.

"What does Franco Rosetti know about pop music?" Bob Jamieson had argued. "He sells ice-cream, doesn't he?"

"He owns a frozen food company," corrected Jim. "A bit different."

"So he's going to freeze and package his darling boy, is he?"

"I don't know about freezing him," replied Jim, "but he'll certainly package him and sell him."

Jamieson rose from his chair. "Do you mind if I creep away? I'll leave you to tell them how talented they are."

"Oh *thanks*," said Jim.

"I'll see you about eight in The Woodman," Jamieson added. "And don't forget to bring the new lyrics."

Bury The Rabbit played on and on... and on!

Rosetti didn't seem unduly concerned when Jim suggested that his band needed a little more rehearsal. He was still confident in his ability and he could just see those music press headlines: NUMBER ONE BAND NOT GOOD ENOUGH FOR THEIR SCHOOL DANCE.

And as Jim gave his pep talk, Franco Rosetti lurked in the background, saying nothing and jangling the keys to his van.

Jim eventually left the hall and found Terry Smith scuttling up the corridor towards the school's main exit.

"What are you doing here?" he asked, firmly.

"I was watching them play," said Terry.

"And?" Jim was curious.

"They're useless!"

"You think so?"

"Rosetti can't sing."

"You could do better, could you?" laughed Jim.

"Much!"

The two walked on to where Billy was waiting for his elder brother.

"Come on!" he yelled, raucously. "Where've you been?"

"They just need a bit more practice, that's all," said Jim.

"And they'll get it, won't they?" replied Terry, bitterly. "With Rosetti's dad's money, they can't fail!"

"Bit of jealously there, lad, don't you think?" Jim winked at him, trying to make light of it.

But for Terry this was far too important. "Yeah, I'm jealous! All that dosh, all that stuff his daddy's bought him... and he's no idea how to use it!" He began to walk off with an arm around his brother's neck. Then he turned.

"'Course I'm jealous!" he said. "Ain't *you*?"

Four

Terry leapt to the trailer window, wiped off the condensation with the back of his hand and gazed out across the campsite. He'd wondered if the wheels he'd heard, churning up the mud outside, belonged to the car bringing his mother home from the hospital. He saw only Levi's van, arriving with the scrap. It was getting dark and car headlamps were beginning to light up the nearby M25. Terry watched these commuters flash by, leaving the busy metropolis for the comfort and respectability of the Kent Weald.

On the far side of the site, Sylvie struggled to her trailer with a bucket of water. Hers was the only authentic Romany trailer remaining here. She and Abi nightly built their fire and ate in the open, and while there were some on the site who found this idea nostalgic or romantic, Terry had no such thoughts. He wanted so much to lead the life of his peers. One day he would have a proper house, with mains water and a bathroom. And he'd do his best to persuade Mum and Dad to move in with him, although he knew they'd refuse. They didn't like houses. Mum hated them. Hadn't she said, many times, that she'd never live like the gorjas? She was happier in a trailer. So he'd make sure that *her* trailer was the best that money could buy, with windows that fitted properly. No draughts in the winter. And Dad would never again have to go on the dole. And Terry would show how much he loved him by buying him a horse. He'd loved his horses. Terry had seen the photo of him riding the black and white mare. He looked so happy in those days. He'd be happy again. And he'd love Terry right back, so grateful he'd be for the horse. And Mum and Dad wouldn't shout at each other any more. There'd be no need for rows... not if they had enough money. It was only the lack of money that caused the rows. And without the rows and without the worries over money and with the windows that fitted properly, Dad would be well again. And Terry wouldn't be forced to go to the hospital to see the man he loved so much withering before his eyes.

"D'you wanna cup o' tea?" Billy slowly approached with a mug filled to the brim. The tea dribbled down the side of it and plopped on to the carpet.

"Oi, careful!" said Terry. "Mum'll kill you."

"D'you think he'll be all right?" Billy was concerned not only at the possibility of his father's death, but at what this would do to his mother. "She won't have to sell dollies outside the bingo hall again, will she?"

Terry shuddered at the idea. The last time they were short of money and Mum had been out selling pegs, she hadn't come home all night. A police cell, followed by a fine in the courts, had left them even shorter.

"Don't want no gavvers round 'ere again," said Billy.

Terry put his arm around his brother's shoulders. "He'll be all right," he said. "Dad's as strong as an ox."

Belcher pumped on his horn as the car pulled up outside. Terry watched his mother climb out and head for the trailer.

"*He's* not coming in with her, is he?" asked Billy.

"Looks like it," Terry replied. "Why doesn't he go to his own trailer and leave us alone?"

Belcher had been good to them, ferrying Mum to and from the hospital every day and making sure that they always had enough to eat. But Terry and Billy felt uncomfortable whenever he was around. He seemed to be taking over. Controlling their lives. Doing Dad's job!

Her face was pale; her headscarf pulled tightly back.

"How is he?" asked Terry.

"About the same," she replied. She turned to Billy. "Make us a cuppa tea, boy."

"Yous ought to go and see him, you know," said Belcher. His huge frame filled the door between the kitchen and 'the room'. He moved slightly to one side, allowing Billy to squeeze through to the stove.

"I *will* see him." Terry almost whispered the words, afraid that anything more audible would constitute a promise. "I'll see him when he's better."

Mother began to remove her coat. "You've got to face it, love," she said, "he may not get..." Her words trailed away. She draped her coat on the back of a chair and covered her eyes with one hand.

Billy lit a gas-ring and placed the kettle on top of it. He silently watched the flames, turning through red to a watery blue.

Five

The class felt silent, listening in awe, amazed at the power behind the voice. He strummed his guitar as he sang:

> "You call on me
> When you are lonely
> Though I know I can only
> Be a friend..."

No one here had ever dreamed that Terry Smith had such talent, least of all Jim Buckley. The cabaret during the last double period before the Easter break was a regular end-of-term occurrence for Jim's form. Some presented short sketches, others told jokes, but rarely did anyone sing. Not even Rosetti could be persuaded to perform without amplification.

Terry finished his song and bobbed his head in a modest attempt at a bow. Most watched him open-mouthed as he returned to his desk, where he began polishing his glasses. Some giggled. Rosetti stared out of the window. No one applauded. The pips sounded, signalling the start of the holiday and they all cheered.

Terry was asked to stay behind as everyone else was dismissed.

"Great voice," said Jim.

"Thanks," Terry smiled.

"Do you fancy doing a little job for me during the holiday?"

"What's that then?"

"I've written a couple of songs. Well, to be precise, Mr Jamieson and I have written a couple of songs."

Terry wondered where this was leading.

"We're going to make some demos."

"Yeah?"

"You'd sing them much better than us."

Terry shrugged. Jim took this to mean that he wasn't interested. "So you won't do it?"

"I'll do it for *you*," replied Terry.

Jim knew what he meant. "Mr Jamieson's all right, you know. His bark's worse than his bite."

Terry lifted his guitar and laid it across his shoulder.

"I'll do it for *you*," he repeated.

Maureen took a short cut through the back of the technology block on her way home. Terry was collecting his bike from the sheds as she passed.

"Give us a ride, superstar!" she called.

Terry almost broke the padlock trying to release the bike quickly, in order to catch up with her.

"If you carry my guitar, you can sit on my crossbar."

She laughed. "I was only joking." She walked to the bus stop and searched her pockets. "Oh, no!" she said. "I've left my bus pass in Ray's bag and he's gone swimming with Scotty."

Terry grinned. "You'll have to walk." He was grateful for the missing pass. It meant he could spend a few more minutes with her.

"It's not too far," she said.

Terry felt unusually confident. "Can I walk with you?"

"If you like."

They passed through the flats on The Belling Estate and into a tidy street of well-kept council houses.

"I was supposed to be going swimming *with* them," said Maureen, "but my gran's got the nurse coming."

She stopped at the crumbling green gate to her house.

"Do you want to come in for a cup of tea?"

"Won't your gran mind?"

Maureen smiled. "Why should she?"

She waited for Terry to padlock his bike to the fence and then led him into the house.

"Is that you, Mo?" Gran called from the kitchen.

Maureen whispered to Terry, "She always says that." Then she called back, "Of course it's me. Who did you think it was?"

Gran appeared in the hall in her wheelchair and peered over the top of her glasses at the visitor.

"This is Terry," said Maureen. "He wants a cup of tea."

"You and me both, love," replied Gran. "Put the kettle on, Mo."

She wheeled herself towards the front room. "Let's have it in the front room. Then I can keep an eye out for the nurse."

Maureen grinned at Terry, who followed her into the kitchen.

"She seems nice," said Terry.

"She's great." Maureen filled the kettle at the sink, plugged it in and pressed the switch. "She's in a lot of pain, but she never complains."

Gran called from the front room, "That stupid nurse is always late!"

Maureen giggled. "Well, she doesn't complain very often, put it that way."

She placed three teabags into the pot and reached up to the shelf for two mugs and Gran's cup and saucer, which she placed on a tray.

"Why do you live with your gran?" asked Terry. He immediately began to worry that she might think he was being too inquisitive.

"My mum's dead."

"Oh!" Terry wasn't sure how to react. "Sorry."

"It's all right. It was a long time ago. She had an accident." She took a bottle of milk from the fridge. "You don't want it in a jug, do you?"

"Er… no," Terry stammered.

She placed the milk bottle on the tray beside the mugs. "She slipped. Or so they say. She was coming home from work and there was a lot of people at the station. And she slipped."

Terry was embarrassed. "That's terrible."

"Gran nearly went mad. She was her only daughter."

"Where's that tea?" Gran called. Perhaps she'd heard. Perhaps she was trying to shut Maureen up.

"Give us a chance," Maureen laughed. "Kettle's not boiling yet." And as an afterthought she called, "Do you want anything to eat?"

"There's some Jaffa Cakes in the blue tin," Gran replied. "That horrible one… with the violets on."

"So what about your dad?" asked Terry. "Where's he?"

"I've no idea," shrugged Maureen. "I don't know and I don't care."

Terry was shocked. "Of course you care. He's your dad."

"I hate him," said Maureen. "And so did my mum."

Terry had never heard anyone speak about their parents like that. Not even Belcher. And *he* had good reason to. His parents had deserted him when he was only eight and if it hadn't been for Terry's Uncle Render, taking him in and bringing him up like one of his own, Belcher would have gone into care.

Maureen put the sugar bowl and a teaspoon onto the tray and decided to change the subject. "You've got a great voice. I couldn't believe it. And it was a brilliant song."

"Thanks. Mr Buckley said so too. I'm going to help him make a demo. One of his songs."

"Really?" Maureen was surprised. "I didn't know he wrote songs."

"But don't say anything, will you?" Terry added, quickly. "I don't want anyone to know."

"Of course I won't," she said. "You sing much better than Ray, you know."

Terry began to panic. "Don't tell Rosetti, will you? Especially not him."

Maureen laughed. "Don't be daft. I don't tell Ray everything, you know. I don't tell him anything important!"

Terry had assumed that Rosetti and Maureen would know everything about each other. They'd been together for ages.

"We talk about music and the band and clothes and that." She giggled. "And we talk ever such a lot about Ray Rosetti." She laughed, loudly.

Terry didn't. If Ray Rosetti knew that Terry Smith had been laughing about him...! He daren't think about it.

Maureen saw the look on his face. "We have a good time together," she volunteered. "He's nice. He takes me to places I've never been before. I like him. I like him a lot, but... well... you know. There's nothing in it."

Terry didn't mean to say it. The words slipped out. "He's not nice. I don't know what you see in him."

She poured boiling water onto the teabags. "His dad's loaded, you know."

"I know!"

Maureen noted the bitterness. "It's not everything, you know, Terry. I mean… it's nice, I admit. *Very* nice. But being well-off brings its own problems, you know." She shrugged. "Or so Mr Rosetti keeps telling me."

"It's everything to *me!*" replied Terry. "*I'd* like a few of the problems that go with being rich!"

Maureen smiled at him, mischievously. "You *wouldn't* like it."

Terry grinned at her. "Wouldn't I just? I wanna be stinking rich. And unbelievably famous!"

"A superstar, right?"

"A megastar!" He suddenly became very serious. "I hate being a nobody. I want people to know my name. I want them to buy my music and put pictures of me on their bedroom walls."

Maureen laughed. "I wouldn't want to put pictures of you on *my* bedroom wall. I'd have nightmares."

"You would. You wait 'til I'm famous!"

Maureen reached up for the blue cake tin.

"I'll wait," she said.

"She'll go mad!" guffawed Rosetti as he pushed his wet towel into his bag. He held up Maureen's bus pass for Scotty to see. "Look! She would have had to have *walked* home!"

They decided to take it to her; tease her about it, have a laugh. Besides, they both fancied a cup of tea with Gran, who always made them so welcome.

As soon as they'd entered the street, Scotty recognised the bike. He stared at Rosetti, wondering why he hadn't reacted.

"Nurse is still there," said Rosetti. "The old girl won't be pleased to see us if she's having her legs done."

The nurse left the house, passed the bike and got into her car.

Rosetti looked at Scotty. Then at the bike. Then back at Scotty.

"I *thought* you hadn't realised," said Scotty. "That's Terry Smith's bike."

It took a few seconds to sink in... then Rosetti froze before raising a clenched fist and punching it against the palm of his left hand. He stared at Scotty with rage-filled eyes. "Right!" he fumed. "That's it! He's had it! And so has she!"

Six

Jim had arranged to meet Terry on the path which led to the campsite. Terry, who seemed excited about recording the demo, talked incessantly as they approached the trailers. Jim was nervous. His preconceived ideas about gypsy camps were, in part, valid. There was plenty of mud, piles of twisted metal and rusty car chassis. Dogs barked and growled at him as he passed each trailer and one old mongrel leapt at his heels. Terry kicked out at it, sending the overweight dog sprawling on its side.

"He's great, that one," laughed Terry. "He don't like gorjas."

"Am I a gorja, then?" asked Jim.

"Anyone not a traveller is a gorga," replied Terry, raising his eyebrows at his teacher's ignorance. "Yeah, you're a gorga."

Controlled aggression sat on the faces of the men and women they passed and they glared at the intruder, wondering who he was and what he wanted. This was gypsy territory, the world of travellers, where outsiders were rarely welcomed.

Inside, Terry's trailer seemed surprisingly spacious: four separate rooms, all spotlessly clean and adorned with ornaments of china, of glass, of silver, but mostly of brass. On every available surface were framed photographs: grandparents, uncles, nephews, cousins and babies. Jim's eye caught a painting on the wall. A magnificently decorated Romany caravan, horse drawn.

"D'you like it?" asked Terry's mother. "*I* painted that. Only by numbers... but *I* did it."

She welcomed him immediately and, although reticent about her own life and her husband's health, she made Jim feel at ease and able to ask what he'd come to ask.

Of course she didn't mind Terry making a demonstration record. "It'll keep him out of trouble, won't it?" and "Couldn't you take

Billy with you too?" and "Where is this place, then? Over the water?" and "Can he really sing, my Terry?"

Jim left the site liking the woman considerably more than he'd hoped. She was gentle and obviously cared greatly for her kids. Moreover, she'd welcomed a stranger into her home without a second thought, which was more than Jim's own mother would have done. And this was the woman he might have dismissed many a time, with a flick of the hand, not noticing the eyes, as she tried to sell him lucky heather at the tube.

Maureen was expected at eight. "Don't be late," Ray had said, and she wasn't. She knew he'd take her somewhere special and she'd eaten little, hoping it would be to the Chinese.

"Enjoy yourself, darling," her gran had told her. "You're not sixteen every day."

She pressed the bell and waited. Rosetti's father opened the door and was, she felt, particularly cold. He wasn't smiling, nor did he greet her with the usual kiss on the cheek.

"Happy birthday, Maureen," he said, flatly.

"Shall I go up?" she was about to ask him. She always went straight up to Ray's sitting room. But Franco indicated that she should wait in the lounge.

"In here, love. He shouldn't be long."

She wondered if Ray had planned some big surprise. Maybe he'd gathered all their friends together upstairs for a surprise party.

Mrs Rosetti decided to leave the room as soon as Maureen entered. "Well, what have *you* been up to?" she asked, not waiting for a reply.

Ray entered, wearing his scruffiest jeans and an un-ironed shirt. So we're not going out tonight, thought Maureen. And obviously there was no party. Ray would rather be seen dead than appear like this in front of his friends. She was disappointed. He carried no flowers, no present, no card. Surely he couldn't have forgotten her sixteenth? He'd been making a fuss about it for weeks.

"Hi!" she smiled. She eyed him up and down. "Well, *you've* made an effort tonight, haven't you?" she giggled, trying not to show her disappointment.

"I really can't believe you've had the nerve to turn up," he hissed.

At first she thought it must be some kind of a joke, but when she saw the look in his eyes, her face paled. She wanted to say, "What d'you mean?" but the words refused to come out.

"Been seeing the pikey behind my back, have you?"

Suddenly she knew.

He sneered at her. "How long's it been going on, then?"

"Oh, Ray," she tutted. "Don't be stupid."

"I saw him," he mumbled. The words were choking in his throat. "I saw his bike outside your house!"

"He came in for a cup of tea."

His delivery became even more venomous. "And what else?"

She couldn't believe what she was hearing. "Oh, please! He walked me home, Ray. You had my bus pass!"

"Give over! Little Miss Innocent!" He was trembling.

"Ray…" she tried to reason with him.

"How could you go off with a pikey?" he yelled.

Then as he raised his hand to her, she flinched. And he knew, immediately, that he'd gone too far.

"Right!" she said, coldly. "I'm not having *that*!"

She brushed past him and stormed into the hall. He followed her.

"Maureen! You get back here!" he demanded.

Franco Rosetti appeared at the top of the stairs and tried to calm his son. "Now, come on, Ray. Leave it, boy."

Ray Rosetti sneered, glaring at Maureen. "Yeah. He's right. You're not worth it."

"I think it'd be better if you left, don't you, Maureen?" Franco called down, sheepishly.

Maureen glared, first at the father, then at the son. Then she left, slamming the street door behind her. Passing the blue Mercedes in the drive, she slumped at the side of the Rosetti van and sobbed.

How could he? How could anyone be so cruel? The tears were short-lived: her distress was quickly replaced by a cold determination not to repeat history. She remembered her father's cruelty, her mother's tears. There would be no replay.

Seven

At first, Bob Jamieson disapproved of Terry Smith's presence in the recording studio, but on hearing the boy's voice he flashed a smile of acceptance at Jim.

"Bit better that you, isn't he?" he said.

"Just a bit," laughed Jim.

Terry recognised the name of the record producer immediately. Keith Bell had been the producer of Billy Druid's top ten hit, *Blue On Blue*.

"That was a great track," said Terry.

Keith naturally took to the lad straight away and was determined to get the best result he could from the song, encouraging Terry through the talkback system.

Terry adjusted the headphones and cleared his throat. He gave a thumbs-up sign through the glass partition to the control room, where Jamieson and Buckley smiled back, encouragingly.

"Okay. Standing by," said Keith. "Let's go for a take."

There was a pause.

Terry listened to the intro, then sang…

> "He's circling way up in the sky
> Reaching out for the sun
> Ten thousand eyes pursuing him
> Since the fall has begun.
>
> Who let the sparrow die,
> Now that he's learned to fly?"

His lone voice, high and haunting, filled the control room. Terry was the only one able to hear the backing as he sang into the microphone.

He knew it was only a demo. He knew it didn't matter if the end result wasn't perfect, but it was important to give it everything he'd got. Terry Smith was, for just one afternoon, standing out from the crowd in the way he *wanted* to stand out. He'd become the focal point for three adults, two of whom he respected. And even the third had smiled at him. Jamieson had actually smiled at him! And all because he could sing!

Keith Bell brought up the guitar track a little. Then the drums.

"Not bad," said Jamieson.

"Not bad?" grinned Keith Bell. "He's brilliant!"

Terry's voice was sounding better with every line of the song...

"Thinking he can take it,
Hearing crowds upon the ground jeering
Though he thinks that he can make it...
He never will!"

Jim had slept soundly, content in the knowledge that Terry Smith had given 'Sparrow' everything he'd got. It had been a great day in the studio and Keith Bell had delighted them all by saying that it was one of the best demos he'd ever produced.

The phone rang early.

"Hi, Jim. It's Keith Bell," the voice announced. "I've been talking to somebody about your boy."

Jim was hardly awake, particles of sleep still holding his eyelashes together. "My boy? Terry Smith do you mean?"

"The A&R man from Sloop Records will see you. When can you get there?"

"How about two minutes ago?" Jim laughed.

"Tomorrow morning," said Keith. "About ten, with one of those CDs I ran off for you."

They tried not to get too excited as they waited in Sloop Records' palm-filled reception, sipping slot machine coffee from polystyrene cups. An overweight, grey-haired businessman in a pinstriped suit sat opposite.

"It'll all come to nothing," Bob Jamieson whispered to Jim. "He won't like it."

Jim Buckley understood the playing down. It was the best way to avoid disappointment. After all, success in the pop industry couldn't be this easy. Their first song. Their first demo. Their first visit to a record company. But just *supposing*, he thought. Already he could imagine his record on the radio; see it entering the charts. He was giving up teaching, moving from a flat to a detached house, swapping his Mini for a Mercedes.

"Anything's possible in the business," said the fat man as he leaned forward and offered a plump, ring-covered hand to Jim. "Joe Fisher," he said.

Jim and Bob introduced themselves. "We're here to see the A&R man," explained Bob.

"Oh yeah? He's a nice guy," said fat Joe.

Jim told him why they were there. "We're teachers." They told him all about their song writing, their demo and their sixteen-year-old pupil with the incredible voice.

Joe listened, seemingly interested. He'd heard it all before, but he listened, nonetheless. Then it was his turn. "I manage Pete Shannon," he said.

"Really?" replied Bob Jamieson, trying to appear unimpressed, sounding as though he met managers of pop superstars every day of his life.

Jim recalled that Pete Shannon was one of Sloop Records' artists. He'd even bought a couple of his CDs when he was at college.

"They're a bit worried here," Joe went on. "I'm starting my own independent record company and Pete's contract with Sloop is up for grabs next year. They can't do enough for me here at the moment."

"So you aim to take him away from Sloop Records then?" asked Jamieson.

Joe shrugged. "Probably. Depends on what they've got to offer as upfront cash."

The phone at the reception desk buzzed and the secretary picked it up.

"Second floor, room seven," she called to Jim and Bob.

Joe Fisher, aware that he'd impressed them sufficiently, pulled a business card from his top pocket. "If you get no joy here, give me a call," he said. "I can't promise anything, but if your boy's as good as you say he is, I'm prepared to listen."

They knocked on room seven.

"Yeah?" shouted the A&R man. He was talking to someone on the phone in a fake American accent, his feet up on the desk, leaning back in his swivel chair. There wasn't a glance towards Jim and Bob as they entered.

The room was luxuriously furnished with spotlights on the ceiling which carefully picked out framed gold discs on every wall. Most, they noted, were for Pete Shannon. For minutes they stood, feeling uncomfortable, waiting for the phone call to end.

"Don't give me that, pal!" the A&R man suddenly shouted into the phone. "Do you really think I'm that green?" He slammed down the receiver, slid his legs from the desk and stared at the two men opposite.

"Yup?"

He was younger than both of them.

"Keith Bell said you'd see us," Jim almost stammered, feeling like a schoolboy in the Head's study.

"Right," he said. "What you got? "

Jim handed him the demo.

They expected to be offered a seat, but he obviously intended to keep this meeting as brief as possible. He swivelled round in his chair and put the CD on to play.

Jim's mouth was dry. Please let him like it, he thought. But in his heart of hearts, he *knew*. His dreams of instant fame and fortune were already beginning to drift away.

The intro started. The man's face was expressionless. As Terry Smith sang, a shiver of excitement shot along Jim's spine, but still the A&R man's face gave nothing away. He switched off the player and swivelled back with the CD in his hand.

"Nope," he said.

"But you haven't listened to it," protested Bob Jamieson.

"I've heard enough," he said. "It's not right for us. Try one of the indie companies." The phone rang and he picked it up. "Yup?"

Jim and Bob left the office.

Joe Fisher had expected the call. Only one demo in a thousand ever caught the attention of Sloop's A&R man. Joe also knew that unless there was something really special about the boy, there was little chance of him taking Terry Smith under his own management wing. But he *was* looking for new talent for his independent record label and he'd promised to listen to the demo.

At first sight of the boy, flanked by his teachers, Joe stifled a laugh. He was fairly good-looking behind those appallingly unfashionable glasses, but with the mousy, badly cut hair, the cheap jeans and the dirty, scuffed trainers, Terry Smith looked no inch a pop star. Joe spoke kindly to him, asking questions, trying to extract some information about his background. Terry was almost monosyllabic, frightened that in saying too much he might reveal that he was a gypsy. *That* had to be hidden at all costs. It had nothing to do with his singing; nothing to do with this probing gorja. If Terry Smith were to make it to the top, it would be *in spite* of his background, not *because* of it.

Joe ran the CD three times in a row, not saying a word between plays... but Jim noticed the thrill in the fat man's eyes. His smile broadened to a wide grin as the song reached its third conclusion.

He looked at Terry. "You're no Pete Shannon, lad," he said. "But you'll do. Let's give it a go."

Longing for a celebratory drink, yet aware that he'd promised to deliver Terry back to the campsite, Jim arranged to meet Bob Jamieson later that evening. He drove the boy along the M25, unable to contain his bubbling excitement. Terry seemed amazingly cool.

"Aren't you pleased?" asked Jim.

"Of course I am. It's what I've always wanted."

There was a long silence.

"Do you want me to come in and tell your mother?"

"*I'll* tell her," said Terry.

"Don't you go getting any ideas about leaving school yet though, Terry," warned Jim. "Exams first, eh?"

"What do I need exams for?" asked Terry.

Jim was unsure if he was serious. "To fall back on, of course," he said. "It's not secure you know, pop singing. If it all goes wrong, you'll need those qualifications to get a proper job."

"A proper job?" Terry turned his nose up at the prospect.

Jim pulled up outside the campsite and as Terry climbed out, he wound down the window. "Think about it, Terry," he said, seriously.

"I've been thinking about it for years," Terry replied. "And *nothing*'s going to stand in my way!" He was about to walk off but stopped, then turned and popped his head through the open window. "Mr Buckley... thanks!"

As Jim turned the corner, he saw Maureen walking in the direction of the campsite. She recognised his car and waved.

He waved back.

What's *she* doing here?" he wondered.

Eight

Terry's life seemed to change within the space of a few days. It was easier to dream, now that the dream appeared tangible. And the more that he dreamed, the less he felt trapped, which made the site seem less muddy, the trailer not quite so claustrophobic.

Between visits to Joe's London office, he played his guitar with renewed fervour, creating new songs, jotting down ideas. And Maureen was always there to encourage him.

Jim was disappointed, but not surprised, to find that Terry hadn't returned to school after the Easter break. There was a note in the register, coldly informing him that Terry Smith had found employment and wouldn't be taking his exams.

"Do you blame him?" grinned Bob Jamieson when Jim showed him the note. "I wish I were in his shoes."

Jim called Joe Fisher on his mobile.

"It's got nothing to do with me," protested Joe. "That's entirely up to Terry. And quite honestly," he added, "I don't think it's got anything to do with you either. He's not a kid. He's a young man with a bright career ahead of him... just so long as he plays his cards properly."

Jamieson whispered in Jim's ear, "Ask him what's happening about our song."

"All right. We'll see you on Saturday," said Jim. "Bye."

Jamieson was irritated. "So?"

"He said it was all Terry's idea."

"Jim!" hissed Jamieson. "If you think I'm going to lose any sleep about some pikey quitting school, you've got another think coming! It's our song I'm concerned with."

"We've got to chew over the details on Saturday," said Jim.

Maureen was just leaving the campsite as Jim arrived. He'd noticed the girl's odd behaviour at school. She was usually the centre of attention, always surrounded by friends. Today she'd not spoken to anyone. Her split with Rosetti was obvious to all. He looked unwell, his eyes sunken and dark. Not once had they glanced at each other during registration and at break Jim had seen him in the library, seemingly engrossed in a text book. His cronies had temporarily abandoned him... even Scotty, who now spent every minute of his time with his girlfriend, Tracey.

"Hello, sir," said Maureen. "Come to see Terry?"

Jim realised the girl knew everything.

"He's about to have his tea," she said. "That's why I'm leaving."

Jim forced a smile and headed for the Smiths' trailer.

Mrs Smith welcomed him like an old friend. She'd been delighted with Terry's news and couldn't thank Jim enough for his help.

"Is he gonna be famous, sir?" asked Billy.

Jim knew how difficult it would be to break the euphoria, but he tried, nevertheless, to put the facts, pure and simple, to a sullen Terry and his attentive family.

"That's daft," said Mrs Smith, finally. "If my Terry stays on at school and this record's released, how's he gonna push it? If he's too busy with his exams to help promote the thing, what happens then?"

"He needs those qualifications," sighed Jim. "Can't you see? There are thousands of lads out there, all in the same position as Terry, all trying to get record deals..."

"I've got one!" snapped Terry. "That's the difference!"

"He may have success with this record," Jim continued, "but then again, he may not. *Then* what?"

"He can make another one," countered Billy.

"I know thousands of unemployed people with qualifications," exaggerated Terry, and as an afterthought, "I hate school!"

Mrs Smith decided, politely, to bring the conversation to a close. "I've got to get tea ready, Mr Buckley," she said. "I'm going to the hospital tonight."

Belcher thumped loudly on the trailer door and entered. "Ain't yous finished tea yet?" he asked, ignoring the presence of the stranger.

"This is Mr Buckley," explained Terry's mother. "Him what got Terry into the singing."

"*Is* it now?" said Belcher. There was no handshake. No smile. He turned and spoke gruffly to Terry. "Come on. You're old enough to get your own tea. Your mother'll be late."

"I'm sorry," said Jim. "I was just leaving." He felt intimidated, afraid... and he wondered what role this bear-like man played in Terry's life. "Will you think about what I've said, Mrs Smith?" he added as he headed for the trailer door.

"I'll think about it, Mr Buckley," she replied, softly. "But it's Terry's life, ain't it?"

Terry followed Jim from the trailer. "I'll see you off, sir."

The two walked in silence, threading their way through the mud and clothes lines, towards the main gate. Jim had said all he'd needed to say.

"I know you're only thinking about what would be for the best, sir," said Terry. The sullen expression had been replaced by one of frustration. "But you're wrong. It's not what's best for *me*. You... you don't understand." He was trying to teach the teacher. "You could never understand!"

"Try me," replied Jim, kindly.

There was so much that Terry wanted to say. If only he could speak to Jim in the same way that he spoke to Maureen. He wanted to tell him how grateful he was for the introduction to Joe. How grateful he was for not being treated any differently from the other kids, just because he was a traveller. How grateful he was to the teacher for always standing up for him when the likes of Rosetti started the name calling.

Grateful! Grateful! Always grateful!

Gorjas would never understand!

How could they?

"I can't," he said, and he turned and walked back to his trailer.

Joe Fisher pushed the contracts across the desk to Terry. "Get your father to sign there," he said. "And here. And this one. Both copies."

"Can't my mum do it?" asked Terry.

"It doesn't matter to me who signs them, just so long as they're signed."

Terry flicked through the papers. He couldn't understand a word.

"It's a standard contract," said Joe. "Don't worry. I won't bleed you."

Terry's new manager opened his cocktail cabinet. "A drink, eh? What do you want?"

"Nothing," replied Terry. "Unless you've got some coke."

Joe smiled and reached for a bottle of Perrier.

Terry was keen to get straight down to business. "What about the song, then? You said you wasn't sure."

"Oh, I'm sure, all right," said Joe. He poured himself a large scotch on the rocks. The ice cracked as he brought the glass to his desk. "I'm sure it's not right for *you*. It's a good song, but it's too country and western."

Terry nodded. "Right."

"You wouldn't stand a chance with it." He took a sip from his glass. "I'll have to look around. Got to be a ballad, though. I've no doubts about that."

"What about one of *my* numbers?" asked Terry.

Joe was mildly surprised. "I didn't know you wrote."

"I can't write it down. The *music*, I mean..." said Terry, "but I've got some good ideas."

Joe smiled. "Well... make a recording for me and I'll see if there's anything we can use."

Terry's thoughts immediately turned to Jim Buckley. How would he take the news that his song wasn't going to be used? He wondered if he should go and see him and break it to him gently, tell him that it wasn't his fault and that it was Joe's idea... say that he was sorry and how grateful he was for everything. He decided he couldn't do it. He wondered why he should! Anyway, it was Joe's problem. He'd leave it to him. It was time to stop worrying about Jim Buckley. It was time to stop being continually grateful. He had his career to concentrate on. And from now on... that was all that mattered!

Joe's phone call came as a bombshell. Jim had arranged to meet Bob at The Woodman for a lunchtime pint, before they set off for London. The phone dragged him from the shower.

"It's Joe. Got a bit of bad news, I'm afraid."

Jim didn't know what to expect. "There's nothing wrong with Terry, is there?"

"No. He's fine. Like a kid with a new toy."

Then Jim knew. It had to be the song.

"It's 'Sparrow'."

"You want a rewrite on it?"

"I'm sorry. No," said Joe. He sounded genuinely upset about giving the news. "It's just not right for Terry."

"We've got plenty more material we can work on." Jim was clutching at straws.

"I think I've got something else lined up," explained Joe.

"Another writer?"

"Yes."

Jim could hardly speak.

"You see, Terry's decided to write his own stuff."

"I see."

He didn't see. He didn't understand how the boy could do this to him. He hung up. How was he going to tell Jamieson?

Nine

Bury The Rabbit had gathered at the Rosetti home because Franco wanted to talk to them. The Leroy twins, in their usual, self-contained manner, sat as one, flicking through magazines from the coffee table, occasionally whispering to each other. Scotty had brought along Tracey and had been dropping hints since their arrival about the girl's talent.

"She can really sing, you know, Ray. Better than Maureen."

Ray Rosetti hadn't shown much interest in the idea and Franco was totally against it.

"No more girls, Scotty," he stated, firmly. "They only cause problems. Now that Maureen's gone, it's just the four of you."

He sent the sulking Tracey into the kitchen to chat with his wife, whilst he talked business.

"I've booked a studio for the seventeenth," he informed them. "No demos this time. We're going for the real thing."

Scotty looked at Rosetti and smiled.

"But you keep it quiet! Right?" Franco went on. "Not a word at school. I'll call your parents and tell them the same. I don't want any more irate phone calls, telling me that the group's interfering with your studies. We'll cross that bridge when we come to it. Right?"

"Right!" said Rosetti Junior.

The Leroys nodded.

"So keep it hush-hush! And that includes you, Scotty."

Scotty looked at him, wide-eyed and innocent.

"I don't want Tracey to know."

"She won't tell anyone, Mr Rosetti," protested Scotty.

"The schoolboy game playing is over, Scotty," threatened Franco. "I'm putting a lot of money into this and I promise you faithfully, one word from you to Tracey and you're dropped! I've already got another drummer lined up, right?"

Scotty fell silent.

"Right?" repeated Franco.

"I won't say a word, Mr Rosetti," said Scotty.

"I think you should record that song you did in class," said Maureen as she led Terry through to the back room.

Terry had arrived at Gran's house with his guitar, his laptop and a bag filled with scraps of paper. His head buzzed with tunes and he couldn't wait to start.

"What, 'Call On Me' ?"

"Yes. It's good," she said.

He pushed the door to, so that Gran couldn't hear them. "First things first," he grinned as he removed his glasses and put them into his shirt pocket. He placed the laptop and the guitar onto the sofa bed and then put his arms around Maureen's waist, pulling her gently towards him.

Terry played it back over and over again:

"Call on me,
You'll find a stranger.
I gotta change,
It's not the same anymore.
I've been down, I've been a loner.
I don't intend staying one, anymore."

"I'll go and make us some cocoa," said Maureen.

"Don't forget me," smiled Gran, as she wheeled herself into the room.

The cushion behind her shoulders was beginning to slip and Terry crossed to her and straightened it.

"Thank you, love." She grabbed his hand. "How's your dad, Terry? Any better?"

"Just the same," he replied. "I've got this awful feeling..."

"He'll be all right," said Gran. That's what people had said to her, when her Ralph was ill, all those years ago. But they were wrong. "You'll see. He'll be all right," she repeated.

There was a brief silence as Terry's mind wandered to that terrible night at the campsite when...

"Does this record man... Joe... know anything about it?" asked Gran. "I mean, if anything should go wrong and you have to go off for a few days. Not that it *will* go wrong, I'm sure, but..."

Terry knew what she meant. "No, I haven't told him. I haven't told him anything about my family. Well, not much anyway."

"He knows you're a gypsy, though?"

Terry looked down at his feet. "He doesn't know we're travellers. No."

"Oh!" said Gran. She was surprised. Surely he wasn't trying to keep *that* secret?

"I don't want him to know. I don't think it's got anything to do with him, do you?"

She smiled at him. "No, Terry. You're right. What's it got to do with anybody?"

Maureen eventually entered with a tray of mugs. "I've put two sugars in yours, Terry," she said.

"He doesn't want any sugar," chuckled Gran. "He's sweet enough."

The cocoa was comforting, reminding Terry of days long past, when he and Billy, dressed in their pyjamas, cheeks burning and smelling of soap, had sat on Dad's knees and had been bounced up and down as he sang to them. Travellers' songs. Songs that Terry couldn't remember now. And they'd giggled and saved their last drop of cocoa until it had gone thickly cold, not wanting to finish it; not wanting to be told it was time for bed. And Terry had asked if he could play hairdressers and had raked forward Dad's Brylcreem-covered hair with his fingers until it had covered his eyes completely, which had made all of them laugh, including Mum.

And he realised that he'd probably never hear Dad sing again. And he knew that he was expected to go and see him; that it was his duty. But how could he make Belcher understand that he just couldn't bear it? The kidney bowls and the nurses squelching along the corridors in their flat-bottom shoes. And the smell of antiseptic, trying to cover but only highlighting the smell of sickness, including that of his father. And he felt so guilty. And bad. Deep down bad. Not at all sweet. Not sweet, Gran. No. Not at all sweet!

Ten

Triumphant Recording Studios were booked for the day and Keith Bell was the producer. Rosetti sang the lyric... and he meant it:

"Got no intention of queuin' for the social
Or windin' up servin' in a burger bar.
I'd bust a gut before I give up losin'
My faith in me, to make it as a star..."

The Leroy twins joined him,

"And it's easy,
Know what I mean?
Easy!"

Scotty looked on with pride, his drum track already laid down and approved by all.

Keith Bell mixed and remixed until he and Rosetti were satisfied with the result. It was the first time he'd taken the reins as a producer in his own right. No co-production on this one, so this recording was as important to him as it was to Bury The Rabbit. And Keith Bell had connections at Sloop Records. He rang and made and appointment.

Maureen was, to say the least, impressed by the luxury of Joe's office-cum-home. She'd never visited this part of London's West End before; never seen the opulent houses which stretched from the bustle of Oxford Street northwards to The Planetarium. Terry led her through a cobbled mews, past neat rows of newly-painted cottages, to a three-storey semi, the detached side of which overlooked a narrow alley.

He pointed up to a tiny window, where the wisteria ceased its climb. "That's his office," he said. "The rest of it is his house."

Maureen sighed. How different this was from The Belling Estate. She and Gran had always considered themselves fortunate not having to live in the flats, with their graffiti-daubed lifts. So often in the past, when she could still walk with the stick, Gran had laughed about her 'lucky legs'.

"Without those, we'd have been put up there," she'd say, pointing to the eighth floor of Toronto House.

Terry pressed a bell and waited.

"Yes?" a voice asked on the intercom.

"It's me, Joe," said Terry.

There was a buzz as the door opened automatically.

"How posh," Maureen wanted to say as they entered Joe's portrait-lined hallway. But she bit her tongue, determined not to be a disappointment to Terry.

Joe was pleased, if somewhat surprised, to meet Maureen. Her name had never been mentioned and the possibility of a girlfriend in Terry's life hadn't occurred to him. He realised how little he knew about Terry Smith's private life. He knew there was a younger brother and that both parents were living, but from the address he'd been given, he couldn't picture what sort of home the boy came from. Letters were addressed to him 'c/o Jane at Berryfield'.

Jane owned the land, collected the rents and allowed the use, occasionally, of the telephone. From here the electricity was generated and, for a few pence, a shower arranged. 'Berryfield' looked good on paper, but Terry's appearance, in his well-worn clothes, belied the suggestion that his lifestyle was in any way grand. The more Joe had questioned him, the less information Terry had offered. But now there was Maureen. And with a little coaxing, Maureen would tell him all he wanted to know.

From the Persian rug on which she stood, Maureen gazed at the pictures, the curtains, the lamps. Her eyes darted from one luxurious item to another, her mouth slightly agape, looking for all the world, thought Joe, like a modern day Eliza Doolittle on her first visit to Higgins's place. She was suddenly aware of her awkwardness, her desire not to seem too impressed… and her feeling of not belonging. Most of all, she was aware of her shoes. Had she wiped them thoroughly before entering? Or had she brought dirt or mud or, please no, anything else from the street onto the Persian?

"Make yourselves at home," said Joe. "I'll go and make us some coffee."

Make yourselves at home. Maureen grinned within, but sat, saying, "Thank you."

Joe seemed pleased with the songs which Terry had copied onto a CD and he chose two, having no doubts that they were chart material. Terry was delighted that his debut number would be Maureen's favourite, 'Call On Me'. His mind dashed back, fleetingly, to the cross country run: to Jamieson, to Scotty, to Rosetti… and to the cut lip. And he glanced at Rosetti's ex-girlfriend, now sitting beside him on the sofa… and he laughed at the irony of it all.

"I'll get these songs arranged and book a studio," said Joe. "Just leave it with me." The doorbell rang and he picked up the entry-phone. "Yes?"

"It's Pete."

"Come on up, Pete," said Joe, as he pressed the door-release button.

Terry knew, though Maureen didn't, that 'Pete' was Pete Shannon.

"We'll go," said Terry.

Maureen couldn't understand the hurry.

As they left, Pete Shannon was just climbing the stairs. Terry trembled, excited to be so close to a superstar and Maureen's knuckles whitened as she gripped the banister on seeing the world-famous face.

"Hi!" said Pete Shannon, and he was gone.

Maureen, eyes widening, mouthed to Terry, "That's Pete Shannon."

"Yes," said Terry, trying to sound cool, "I know. I thought I told you… Joe manages him too." He grinned. "I'm gonna end up like him one day. You watch!"

A list of appointments kept Terry busy all week. There were visits to

Chelsea, Fulham and Knightsbridge for his everyday wear: shirts, jeans and shoes. The hair was cut and slightly streaked.

"Just enough," said Joe, "to catch the studio lights," adding, with a wink, "it's got to look good on *Chartbusters*."

Terry's heart beat faster. This was his dream...appearing on *Chartbusters*, the UK's most important music TV show, which presented the top forty songs from downloads and record sales. He smiled at Joe.

The teeth were noted: they had to be polished (one was in need of a crown). The spectacles were replaced by contact lenses in piercing blue. Fairy Godfather Joe was preparing his male Cinderella for the ball.

Terry stared into Gran's mirror at the handsome stranger who faced him and he was aware for the first time in his life of the true power of money. Maureen stood behind him, gazing at the reflection. She'd never realised he was quite so good-looking.

She laughed, "Well, if you don't make it, at least you've still got the clothes."

He grinned. "I *will* make it. No doubt about it."

Maureen left him, still staring at himself, while she went to the kitchen to prepare Gran's tea.

Terry posed, miming the guitar and noting the newly-whitened teeth as he smiled at the imaginary camera. The country was tuned in to *Chartbusters*, to hear what was at number one. Terry sang:

> "Gotta get myself in line,
> Find the words to say to you,
> Tell you how I feel, 'cause I'm
> Hung up waitin' on you.
> You call on me
> When you are lonely..."

Maureen called from the kitchen, "Terry! Come and help me butter some bread."

Eleven

Rica Stubbs had been offered the Rosetti interview for *GO* magazine's pop page. Having heard a promo of 'Easy', she was sure that it was a sure-fire top-twenty hit, given the right exposure of course… and Rica couldn't wait to meet the man behind the voice. She'd seen the photo of the group, sent with the promo from Sloop Records, and she'd liked what she'd seen.

She wasn't disappointed. Rosetti arrived at five-thirty as arranged, wearing scrubbed denims and trainers. His mother's sunbed had heightened his dark-skinned good looks. He contrived, convincingly, to peer smoulderingly at Rica through the quiff of his gelled black hair, which fell down over his dark brown eyes. And as he answered all her questions, he took care to use his smile whenever he felt he needed to score points.

"So you're still at school?" she asked him.

"That's right." He laughed. "Aren't *you*? You look so young."

She laughed too.

"Yes, I'm still at school," he went on. "Year eleven. Scotty, the drummer, and I are in the same form."

"And the Leroy twins?"

"The year above. I was elected to do the interview."

"Elected?" She raised an eyebrow. "Very democratic."

"We're a team," said Rosetti. "No one person in the band is more important than the other."

"So what happens if the record's a hit?"

"How do you mean?" He smiled broadly, adding, "I *hope* it's a hit."

"What happens about school?"

"I'll probably leave," he replied. "I *am* sixteen."

"And the others?"

"That depends on them. And their parents, of course."

"And if their parents want them to stay on?"

"We'll survive," said Rosetti. "We'll have to do as much promo work as possible during the holidays."

"What sort of school do you go to?" she asked.

"Just an ordinary, rather large high school," he replied. He seized the chance to volunteer information he felt was important to the interview. "We're all working-class boys, you know; council estate etc. It's pretty rough where we live."

"And you want to get away from all that?" She wondered if this was her headline for the article.

"Wouldn't *you*?" said Rosetti. He smiled at her again.

She smiled back. "I *did*!"

They both laughed.

"No, I wouldn't leave my roots," continued Rosetti, still smiling, aware that she was aware of the untruthful hype. "I'm not saying I enjoy poverty, but I couldn't join the jet-set. I could never be part of that. And do you know, Rica," he went on, "there's a lot to be said for people like us. We've got our heads screwed on the right way. I'm sure you know what I mean."

She refused to acknowledge the remark.

"We know what's important in life," he said. "Money isn't really that important."

"And what *is* important to you?" she asked.

He grinned, musing, "What *is* important to me?"

"Yes."

He stared at her. "You're really beautiful, you know," he said.

She held his stare… and then shrieked with laughter.

He was surprised by her reaction.

"Give over!" she cackled. "Where do you think I'm coming from?"

"No, I mean it," he said.

"You want me to write a nice little article about you, more like," she replied.

"And will you?" His eyes were twinkling.

"I may do," she replied, twinkling back. "You'll have to wait and see, won't you, Mr Rosetti?"

Terry lay awake against his will. He knew it was very late, probably the early hours of the morning, as he could hear few cars passing on the M25. He didn't want to reach for his watch for fear of waking Billy, who was breathing deeply and had been asleep for hours. Through the partition which separated them from Mother's bedroom, the sound of her clock ticked in rhythm with his heart. It was hours earlier when he'd heard her crying softly; when he'd wanted to go to her and say, "It's all right, Mum. Don't worry," but didn't, because he knew, deep down, that it probably wasn't.

And besides, it wasn't like the face on the trailer door, when *he'd* cried all night, fearing that the gavvers had come to get him; when Mother had scooped him from his bed and lifted him up, forcing him to touch the shape on the wall which moved only when the wind blew, proving it was just the shadow of the elm tree outside, diseased and crumbling. No, it wasn't like that at all. But he wished it were. He wished he could point to the shadow of the bogeyman and say, "It'll be gone by morning, Mum, then everything will be the same as it was. With you and Dad and Billy and me, all together like before. But a bit different this time, because I'm going to be rich. And you won't have to cry again."

Tomorrow was the beginning of how it was going to be. Tomorrow he was going to make his first record. It would be such an important day and his desire for rest was paramount. He had to sleep! And sleep, as sleep does, kidnapped the conscious state when it was least aware, and in so doing, presented the subconscious as reality.

The coffin was open, his father's eyes staring at him. Romanies he'd never seen, but whose names he'd heard mentioned, passed by, placing small bags of coins at his father's head. Outside the tent in which the coffin lay, dozens sat cross-legged on the damp grass, some crying, a few wailing. Huge bunches of flowers, yellow and red, hung at each corner of the tent, while small, copper vases, also filled with flowers, decorated its entrance.

Terry put his hand into the coffin and touched his father's forehead. It was cold and felt not at all like flesh. His father winked an eye and tried to smile.

"Come to see me at last, eh, Terry?"

"Almost too late, Dad," the boy replied.

"Almost."

The corpse closed its eyes as Belcher covered it with the lid and began hammering in nails.

He turned to Terry. "He's gone, son. I'm your father now."

Then they were all outside a Romany caravan, carrying burning torches. The mourners watched silently as Levi threw his torch inside. Flames licked their way along the curtain until, with a thunderous roar, the whole place was burning. Sparks shot ten feet in the air as Terry watched the caravan crumble and spit.

His father rose up through the flames, shrouded in smoke, and hovered above the mourners. Terry had never seen him look so peaceful, so young. Dressed in his best suit and with the new boots he'd bought for this special day, he smiled down at those watching.

"It's all true," he said. "I promise yous." And he drifted upwards and disappeared.

The heat grew more intense and Terry gasped for breath. He woke, sweat popping from his hair and running down his face. His pillow was soaked, his sheets no better. He sat up in bed and leaned his head against the wall, taking deep breaths and trying to reason with himself that it was only a dream. Just a dream!

I'll go and see him tomorrow, he thought. After the studio.

Twelve

Despite the lack of sleep, Terry arrived at Denson Studios thirty minutes earlier than arranged and found Maureen already waiting for him.

"You got here all right, then?" he asked, taking her hand.

"Easier than I thought," she replied. "I've even been for a coffee."

None of the big stores had yet opened, but the sandwich bars were already dispensing freshly filled rolls to queues of people picking up their lunches before going to work. Terry pushed at the studio door, expecting it to be locked. It wasn't. He was about to introduce himself at the reception desk when Joe appeared, looking, thought Terry, ridiculously casual for a man of his weight, in blue jeans and a pink sweater, the sleeves of which were pushed up to just above the elbows.

"You look..." Terry struggled for the word "... comfortable."

"No point in dressing up on studio days," replied Joe, as he sucked on an unlit cigar. "It's going to be a long, stuffy day in here."

"You don't mind me being here, do you?" asked Maureen.

"Delighted, Maureen," the fat man replied. "Just so long as you don't have any ideas on producing records."

Having shown them the studio, which was far larger than Terry had expected, Joe led them up an iron staircase to the control room, where, sitting at the multi-track machine, pushing buttons, was the producer.

"Hi!" He rose from his seat and shook Terry's hand. "Great song!" he said.

Joe introduced him as Andy Davis. "Andy was the recording engineer on Pete Shannon's last CD, and he knows as much about production as anyone in the business."

"Should do, after all these years," smiled Andy.

There was a crackle on the huge speakers set on either side of the control room and Andy's recorded voice boomed through them.

"Take four!"

Music followed. A mid-tempo drum beat. A piano rose in volume to equal the drums, then sank again to be swamped, almost replaced, by the sound of a wailing saxophone.

"Well?" shouted Andy, above the music. "What d'you think?"

"Cool!" said Terry. "What is it?"

Joe clipped his ear and laughed. "It's the backing track to your song," he said. "What do you think it is? 'Hickory Dickory Dock'?"

Terry's mouth dropped open. "I didn't recognise it at all," he said.

"You wouldn't," replied Andy. "Not after that awful demo I was given."

Terry listened until the song had finished.

"It's brilliant!" he said.

Joe grinned. "You wait until you hear the other track. They weren't easy to arrange, but Andy's worked miracles."

"We recorded them yesterday," said Andy. "A hot bunch of session musicians, including, would you believe, Rick Wain." He ran the track back to the beginning and placed the lyric sheet, neatly typed, in front of him on the control desk. "I'll sing it to you. Show you where to come in."

After a couple of dummy-runs, Terry went down into the studio to start work, and although Joe was both surprised and delighted that Terry seemed to have 'Call On Me' in the can after the third take, Andy went on and on recording until he was completely satisfied with the result.

"Okay, Terry," he said, finally. "Come up and listen."

Terry, his heart thumping excitedly, returned to the control-room and, having received a glowing smile from Maureen and a pat on the back from Joe, sat before the control desk and waited to hear the rough mix of his very first record.

As the introduction started, he reached out for Maureen's hand. His palm was sweaty and he clutched her just a little too tightly. Let it be good, he thought to himself. Let it be a hit.

The first verse began:

> "You call on me
> When you are lonely…"

Terry was surprised at just how good his voice sounded. He knew he could sing, but…

Joe winked at him. "I think you've cracked it, lad!" he said. "It's got HIT stamped right through it!"

"D'you think so?" asked Terry. "Really?"

Joe smiled. "We'll have you on *Chartbusters* within the month."

Rosetti read the review aloud,

BURY THE RABBIT. 'Easy' (Sloop Records)
Pop pap from four schoolboys with their eyes on the charts. Back to the classroom, lads. There's a lot to learn!

The Leroy twins grinned nervously.

"They know nothing!" snapped Scotty. "I hate that paper anyway. They never get it right!"

Franco smiled and reached into his briefcase for the second pop weekly.

"Isn't this the one you usually read?" he asked.

Scotty took the paper and flicked through it, looking for the review section.

"Well?" asked Rosetti, his voice trembling.

Scotty scanned the page. "No. Nothing here." He was nervous, his eyes hardly focusing. Then he saw it! He read it silently.

"Come on!" shrieked Rosetti. "What does it say?"

"I don't believe it," Scotty mumbled.

Rosetti grabbed the paper and read:

A flawless, squeaky-clean production on this debut from schoolboy band, Bury The Rabbit. A trite, up-tempo dance ditty about wanting to be a star. Unoriginal and boring. In short, a hit.

Rosetti glowered and threw the paper across the room.

"It's the 'boring' bit that gets me!" said Scotty. "I mean… how can he possibly say that 'Easy' is boring?"

"He also says it's a hit," laughed Franco, as he picked up the paper and began reassembling the pages. "The hit record! That's what it's all about lads!"

Terry was beginning to tire. His voice had cracked twice in exactly the same place, but Andy continued to direct him patiently, encouraging him to play with the song, to give it more light and shade. The producer preferred this number to the previous one and he wondered if Joe had made the right decision about 'Call On Me'.

"Let's do the third line again," he said. "I'll drop you in."

Terry listened through the cans, breathing heavily all the time, swallowing, trying to clear the clogged-up feeling from the back of his throat. The red light was on. This time, the voice mustn't crack. He sang:

> "Since then love's gone bad,
> Losin' all we once had.
> Now I've no-one to turn to…"

"White?" asked Joe, his plump fingers hovering over the buttons on the coffee machine.

"Yes please," replied Maureen.

Pretending to tire of listening to the same three lines being repeated over and over again, Joe had used this as an excuse to fetch coffee.

"Coming with me, Maureen?" he'd asked. "I can't carry four."

Now he was alone with the girl who knew everything about the boy in whom Joe was about to invest a great deal of money, the truth was out.

"A gypsy, eh?" said Joe.

"A traveller. Yes," said Maureen. She sighed. "Oh dear. I'm not sure if I should've told you." She looked worried. "Perhaps you ought not to say anything, Joe."

"Don't worry, my dear," he replied. "Our little secret. I won't say anything."

He smiled. Maureen thought that the smile was genuine. But had she looked into the fat man's eyes at that very moment, she might have read a different story.

They sipped coffee and relaxed as best they could, and Andy started the playback.

"You understand, Terry," he said, "it's only a very rough mix."

They listened excitedly. Terry was silent.

Maureen lightly punched his arm. "Well, superstar? What do you think?"

"I think it's brilliant," said Terry. "I can't believe it."

The phone rang and Andy picked it up.

"Phone call for you, Terry," he said. "In reception."

Terry was surprised. "Nobody knows where I am," he said, "except..."

His mouth felt dry. He calmly and slowly walked to the reception area and Maureen followed him.

He could hardly make out the gabbled words.

"It's Billy," was all he heard. Then a choking, muffled sound. A long pause. Then again, "Hello, Terry? It's me. Billy. I'm at the hospital."

Terry began to feel faint. His chest tightened. One leg trembled. He couldn't keep it still. He held the receiver away from him at arm's length, trying to hold back the news. He didn't want to hear it. Not yet. He was about to leave for the hospital, anyway. As soon as he'd finished at the studio. A train from Charing Cross... and then that green bus... he couldn't remember the number... what was that number?... that green bus... that would take him straight there. Right to the hospital door. He'd worked it all out. He'd go into the ward and he'd pass all the coughing, hollow-faced men, and he'd go up to his father's bed. And he'd see his father sitting up and smiling and looking healthy... and he'd say, "Sorry I didn't come earlier, Dad. I *meant* to. *Kept* meaning to. It's not that I don't love you, Dad. I *do*. But..." and still he held the phone away from him, the muscles in his arm stiffening as, in the distance, he could hear Billy's voice, sobbing now and saying, "Terry? Are you there? Can you hear me?"

I don't want to hear you, thought Terry. Please don't tell me.

Maureen took the phone from his curled fingers.

"Hello, Billy? It's Maureen," she said.

"Not yet," said Terry. "Please… not today!"

Maureen half-whispered into the receiver. "Oh, Billy. I'm so sorry. I really am. Yes, yes of course. Yes, I'll tell him."

Thirteen

Maureen stood in the girls' toilets, idly running the brush through her hair. It was the end of the first week of the new term and things were very, very different at school. Although there'd been no sign of Ray Rosetti, nor of Scotty, Maureen's thoughts were entirely on Terry. She wondered how he and Billy were coping with their tragedy. Unlike most of her school friends, she knew what it was like to have to come to terms with the death of a parent. She thought back to the prayers she used to say in those last few minutes before sleep, and to the times when the chicken bone broke in her favour, allowing her a wish. And those prayers and those wishes had always been the same. "Don't let her die." She remembered the panic that used to cramp her stomach when she'd thought, what would happen if...? But it *had* happened. And it had happened to the person she'd loved most in the world. But she'd got over it. She'd never forget her mother. Never. But the pain had gone. And so would Terry's, in time.

Through the mirror, Maureen saw the door open. Tracey entered, carrying her bag in one hand and a newspaper under one arm.

"Oh, *there* you are, Mo," she said. "You gonna walk down the road with me? I ain't got enough money for the bus."

Maureen cursed inwardly. She wanted to be alone. The last person she felt she could talk to now was Tracey. But here she was, tossing her red hair and obviously having no intention of leaving Maureen's side until they reached The Belling Estate.

"So why wasn't Scotty in school?" Maureen asked.

Tracey smiled. "He's talking business with Ray, isn't he? It's tomorrow morning and they haven't sorted out what they're gonna say yet, have they?"

"Sorted what out?" Maureen wasn't in the slightest bit interested.

Tracey stared at her through the mirror. "You don't know, do you?"

Maureen turned to face her. "Know what?"

"They're on the radio tomorrow morning. Radio Viscount. Doing an interview with Robbie Jones."

Maureen turned back to the mirror. "Really? I never listen to Viscount."

"Oh, you should!" enthused Tracey. "He's ever so good is Robbie Jones. And he's already played their song a couple of times. He reckons it'll be a hit. Well, it will, won't it?"

"Their song?" At last Maureen understood.

"Yeah," replied Tracey. "They wanted to keep it all quiet. Mr Rosetti told them to. I was the only one who knew," she added smugly. "But now it's all out in the open, with the reviews, isn't it?" She picked up the paper, which she'd placed on the top of her bag. "Have you seen them by the way?"

"Er… yes," said Maureen, not wanting to see Rosetti's name in print, realising she'd have to react favourably, and knowing that she couldn't.

"Weren't they good? Well, *one* of them was. *Quite.*"

"Yes," said Maureen.

"You all right, Mo?" Tracey looked at her through the mirror. "You look a bit funny. You all right?"

"Yes," replied Maureen. Then, "No, not really. I've got a bit of a headache. Look, would you mind if I got the bus home, Trace? I don't fancy walking."

"Oh," said Tracey. "That's a shame."

"Sorry." Maureen headed for the door. "Sorry, Trace. I'll see you Monday, okay?"

She left hurriedly.

Tracey had the mirror to herself. She ran the brush through her long, red hair and grinned at her reflection.

Maureen got up early and frantically searched for Viscount on her radio. What she'd said to Tracey was true. She never listened to Robbie Jones, but she knew she'd have to today. She'd have to face up to the fact that Bury The Rabbit had released a CD and that it was being given air-time.

Gran joined her, wheeling herself into the front room, with buttered toast for both of them sitting on her lap. She'd always liked Ray and Scotty and she missed their visits. Oh, she liked Terry too. Terry was a nice boy. But he didn't spend as much time as Ray and Scotty used to, listening to the stories of when *she* was young and ambitious. Yes, she liked Ray and Scotty and she was pleased they were on the verge of success.

"What's the record *like*, Mo?" she asked. "Is it good?"

"I don't know, Gran," Maureen replied. "I haven't heard it yet."

"In just a few minutes," said Robbie Jones, "I'll be chatting to Ray Rosetti. He's the lead singer of a band calling themselves 'Bury The Rabbit' and this is their first single…"

Rosetti's voice sang out,

> "Didn't take to schoolin';
> Got no interest…"

Robbie's production assistant led Scotty and Rosetti into the studio, where the music continued to play. Robbie Jones looked up at them and smiled. "Hi, lads!" he said.

Scotty whispered to Rosetti, "It's *live*, don't forget. So watch what you say."

At home, the Leroy twins looked at each other and grinned. Their record sounded great on radio. Tracey bounced up and down, excitedly, on her sofa, giggling. Maureen smiled at Gran and turned up the volume.

And Terry stared into the coffin, with clouded eyes, at the man in the smart suit and new boots.

Fourteen

Levi didn't like the look of the stranger who'd entered the public bar. Sunday lunchtime at The Three Stars had been the same for as long as the travellers could remember and everyone who used the pub knew that the saloon bar was for gorgas and the public bar was for gypsies. Naturally, somebody just passing through and wanting a quick pint couldn't possibly have known, but this one *wasn't* just passing through. Levi was sure of that. The questions were in his eyes. He wasn't a gavver, but he had the look of one. He could have been a reporter from the local paper, but Levi thought he knew all those by sight. All the local gavvers and reporters were well known since that trouble at the campsite, when Mick Mahoney had set his dog on the gavvers who'd come to arrest him. That was the day when Joshua Smith had had his heart attack. For weeks afterwards, the campsite was teeming with gavvers and journalists, leading to even more trouble. Then the RSPCA had been called in for some reason.

"Must've thought that Mick Mahoney's dog had been starved and fancied a gavver for his dinner," Abi had joked. But the joke began to wear thin when stories started to appear in the press about the squalor of the gypsy camp.

"All lies!" Abi had yelled, when someone had read the story to him. "All lies!"

Anyway, Mick Mahoney wasn't even a gypsy. He was a tinker. And unlike the rest of them, he'd spent most of his adult life slammed up in the starry. Though that was no reason for slamming him up this time, for something he hadn't done.

"I'm sorry to bother you," said the stranger.

A few of the gypsies looked up from their beers and stared at him.

"What d'you want?" asked Levi, aggressively.

"I don't know if you can help me…" continued the stranger. He tried to avoid the eyes by gazing at the wood panelling behind Levi's head. "I'm a writer and…"

"What d'you mean, writer?" asked Levi. "You mean you're a reporter?"

Abi's youngest son leapt to his feet, sending a wash of beer across the table. Big Jimmy, as they called him, was the tallest of them all, unshaven and looking much older than his seventeen years. His trade as a roofer had given him huge biceps, which, decorated in tattoos, he always displayed and continually flexed.

"I hope you ain't gonna write nuffin' about me, mate!" he said.

The stranger was terrified.

"Hold on!" interrupted Abi. "How much you gonna pay us?"

The stranger began to tremble. "Look, I'm sorry," he said. "I didn't want to cause a fuss.

"You won't!" growled Levi. "Not if you disappear, you won't!"

Big Jimmy sat down and returned to his beer swilling.

The others stared at the stranger, who decided it was time to leave.

Travelling through the high street which led to the M25, the stranger stopped when he saw a florist taking in his last tray of bedding-plants.

"You've only just caught me before closing," said the florist. "Forgotten the wife's birthday, have you?"

"How did you guess?" He pointed to a bunch of cellophane-covered red roses in a plastic bucket. "I'll have those."

As the florist wrapped the dripping stems, the stranger made what appeared to be polite conversation.

"Do you open every Sunday?"

"Only mornings," replied the florist. "Unless we've got a lot to get ready for Monday. Then we don't open at all."

"Weddings and things?"

The florist laughed. "Not many weddings on a Monday. Plenty going to the church, but not to get married."

The conversation was heading in the direction the stranger had hoped it would.

"You're not busy tomorrow, then?"

"Only *one* tomorrow. A big one, mind you. Me and the missus were up with the sparrow this morning."

"Do you mind if I ask you something?" said the stranger.

"Ask me what you want, mate." The florist handed him his flowers. "So long as it's not how much profit I make on a bunch of red roses." He laughed.

"Is it a gypsy funeral?"

The florist looked at him, trying to weigh him up. Was this guy a gypsy? You couldn't really tell nowadays. Lots of gypsies had gone away, got good jobs, prospered. They only returned for the funerals.

"That's right," was all he said. He took the stranger's money and gave him his change.

"I'd love to see it," said the stranger. "They're usually quite spectacular, aren't they?"

So he wasn't a gypsy.

"This one will be," replied the florist. He pointed across the road to a closed café. "Sit in The Greasy Spoon with the OAPs if you want to see it. It passes about half past two. Should be a good one."

"Where's it heading for?"

"Saint Barnabas' for three, right over at Sancton Heath. But I wouldn't go there," he warned. "They won't take kindly to you gawping."

The stranger thanked him and left with the roses. He threw them on to the back seat of his car and drove off, stopping a few yards along the road to use his mobile.

"Well?" asked Joe Fisher.

"Saint Barnabas', Sancton Heath, tomorrow at three o'clock," he replied.

"Well done," said Joe. "You know what to do."

Apart from the old man in the peaked white cap walking his dog, the beach at Bournemouth's Studland Bay was empty. It had rained throughout Saturday night and had continued into this very cold

Sunday morning. Bury The Rabbit arrived in the hired bus followed by the Transit bringing the film crew and its equipment. Rosetti hadn't checked the storyboard in detail, but Franco had discussed his ideas with Max, the director, who'd made a few, important suggestions. All realised that the pop video was almost as important as the record itself, and although this coastal location was to illustrate only the final verse of 'Easy', it would take the whole day to film.

Max looked up at the black clouds and sighed. "We'll be lucky if we get any sun at all today!"

"We'd better!" shivered Rosetti. "This is supposed to be a beach in Antigua."

Before noon, although the clouds had cleared completely and on parts of the beach the sand had dried to a powdery gold, it was still freezing.

"Right!" said Max. "Let's move it!"

Still wearing their overcoats, scarves and gloves as protection against the bitter wind which was blowing in from the sea, the crew began setting up in the sand – school desks and chairs, a large white board and easel and three authentic-looking palm trees.

Bury The Rabbit returned to the bus with Elaine, the make-up supervisor.

Rosetti was pleased he wasn't going to have to be dressed like Scotty and the Leroys, who, in their short trousers, school caps and ties, looked like overgrown infants.

Scotty was irritated. "This is your father's idea, isn't it? We'll all end up looking like a bunch of idiots, while you stand there like Joe Cool!"

"I'm the sex-symbol of this group, Scotty," said Rosetti, without a trace of humour. "If I dressed up like you lot, we'd all lose street-cred."

"But it's all right for *me* to lose street-cred though, isn't it?" snapped Scotty.

Rosetti was firm. "Yes!"

Stan, in charge of wardrobe, tucked and pinned before passing each of his artistes to Elaine, who only needed to cover the Leroys' pimples with powder.

Rosetti's make-up was to take much longer and was less pleasant. Dressed only in shorts, he shivered and cursed as Elaine applied deep-tan body lotion with a cold, wet sponge.

Max knocked and entered, checking to see if Bury The Rabbit was almost ready. "I don't want you outside until it's absolutely necessary, lads," he informed them. "It's a bit nippy, to say the least."

"Just give me a couple more minutes, Max," said Elaine. "I'm nearly done."

Max was about to leave, when Rosetti called to him.

"Yes, Ray?"

"That cameraman…" said Rosetti.

"John Stellar?"

"Yeah."

Rosetti had taken an instant dislike to him from the moment they'd met. On introduction, the cameraman had hardly looked up from his newspaper crossword as he'd mumbled, "Hi."

"Did you choose him?" Rosetti asked.

"I won't work with anyone else on pop videos," replied Max. "He's the best. Why?"

"I don't like him," said Rosetti.

Max was taken aback.

"He's very nice, Ray," interrupted Elaine. "I've worked with him lots of times."

Rosetti flared. "Excuse me! I'm talking to the director, not the make-up girl!"

Elaine felt her cheeks going red. As a freelance make-up artist, she'd worked with hundreds of big stars and she couldn't remember anyone ever speaking to her like that.

The Leroy twins grinned nervously and looked down at their feet, while Scotty gazed out of the window, looking at nothing in particular.

"He couldn't even be bothered to talk to me!" said Rosetti. "Doesn't he realise who I am? Doesn't he realise that it's my father who's paying his wages?"

"It's just his way," smiled Max. He couldn't understand why

Rosetti was getting so worked up. "He's always like that. Even with the big stars. He gives the impression that he doesn't care, but..."

"And *does* he?" snapped Rosetti.

"He cares!" replied Max, firmly. "I'll see you all outside in five minutes!" he added, and he left.

The members of the crew were, at first, enthusiastic about 'Easy' but with replay after replay on the tape machine, they grew bored, then irritated, then finally sick of the song.

The first shot had Rosetti lying on the sand, sunbathing and singing to the camera, while Scotty and the Leroys tore up their school books and threw them into the air.

> "Shoot your promos on Antigua's beaches
> And take me there with you, to feel the sun..."

"Cut!" called Max. Then, "Check the gate!"

John Stellar checked his camera to make sure everything was okay. It was.

Rosetti was dreading the next shot, gritting his teeth as he walked into the sea. The water was freezing; the wind even worse. He closed his eyes and took a deep breath as he courageously allowed the water to rise above his shorts. Then he turned to face the shore, where the lens of the camera was staring out at him.

"Cue music!" shouted Max, his voice battling with the wind, now howling through the sand dunes behind the beach. The tape of 'Easy' started again.

"And action!" he yelled.

Rosetti tried to relax his muscles, which had become knotted with the cold. He consciously stopped his teeth from chattering and strode to the shore, miming,

> "Plug me with confidence, the way you know how,
> 'Til I'm on my way to be the number one!"

He stepped onto the beach, placed his hands behind his head and held his face to the sun. Through the camera's lens anyone could have mistaken Bournemouth for Antigua. Rosetti looked warm and comfortable in the make-believe tropical sunshine.

"Cut!" yelled Max. Then, "Check the gate!"

Elaine hurried across to Rosetti and wrapped a dressing gown around his shoulders. His body shook, his teeth chattered and the tip of his nose was beginning to turn blue.

"I'm freezing!" he stammered.

"Well done, Ray," said Max. "It looked really good."

"Sorry," called John Stellar, from over his camera. "Hair in the gate!"

"What does that mean?" asked Rosetti.

"Sorry, Ray," replied Max. "No good. We'll have to go again."

Rosetti threw the dressing gown at Elaine, glared at the cameraman and walked back into the sea.

The upstairs room of the restaurant, reserved for party bookings, was large enough to seat crew and cast on six separate white-clothed tables and Rosetti made sure he sat as far away as possible from John Stellar.

Stellar looked up from his menu and called across the room to him kindly, "Feeling a bit better now, Ray? Warmed up a bit?"

Rosetti snapped. "No thanks to you, mate!"

The cameraman put down his menu and crossed to Rosetti's table.

"Come on, lad," he said. "Don't be like that. You wanted it to look right, didn't you?"

"It would've looked right on the *first* take, if you'd been competent at your job," replied Rosetti.

John Stellar decided there was no point in trying to communicate with him. He thought of the 'thank you' parties thrown for him by dozens of world famous pop stars and he smiled at this idiot's accusation as he strolled back to his table.

But Rosetti wasn't going to let it rest.

"You couldn't care less, could you? It's just another pop video! Just another group trying to make the charts… and just another fast buck for you!"

Stellar tried to stay calm. He looked at his menu, though he wasn't seeing the words.

Max called across to Rosetti. "That's enough, Ray!"

Stellar mumbled, "I don't have to take this from some jumped-up school kid!"

Rosetti leapt from his seat and hammered his fist on the table. Scotty's empty glass fell over.

"I'm the star of this group, Stellar!" he screamed. "And my father's paying your wages, so just you watch it, or I'll make sure you never work again!"

One of the burlier prop men had heard enough. He calmly crossed the room and grabbed Rosetti around the throat.

"Shut it!" he said quietly as he pushed him back into his chair.

The meal was ordered and eaten in embarrassed silence.

The cars and lorries stretched from Saint Barnabas' right along Heath Drive and into Sancton High Street. The priest had conducted many gypsy funerals but had rarely seen quite so many flowers. The late Joshua Smith was obviously well known and well loved. Heath Drive split the cemetery in two. The old part surrounding the church was, except for a few reserved plots, full. Close to the church itself, a circle of elaborately-carved headstones commemorated the lives and deaths of the Kings, the Moores and the Lees. The graves were well-kept, though some of them were over fifty years old, and freshly-cut flowers had been placed at the foot of each one.

Terry and Billy tried to comfort their mother as they walked behind the coffin, which was carried from the church, through the old part of the cemetery, across Heath Drive (where a policeman had to stop the traffic) and on into the new part. The flowers represented items that had been part of Joshua Smith's life: his tankard, overflowing with beer, his shovel, a pack of cards, the horse he once owned and the truck which had replaced it. The wreath from Terry and Billy, in large letters, spelt DAD.

Terry didn't hear the words; he was conscious only of his mum's stifled sobs and the white, drawn face of young Billy. But he knew it was something about ashes and dust. And as the coffin was lowered, he thought of Epsom Downs and the sunshine and the caravans and the gypsies in their rolled sleeves and the horses, so *many* horses, and the two fortune tellers both claiming to be the real Gypsy Rose Lee. And he knew that it was gone forever. And he wasn't sure which of the tears that rolled down his cheeks were for the loss of his childhood, and which had been caused by the cold wind blowing up from the river to the heath beyond.

And neither was he conscious of the stranger in the old part of the cemetery who was capturing his tears with a telephoto lens.

Fifteen

Joe was playing 'Call On Me' when Terry arrived at the office. There was no mention of the funeral, which was a relief, as Terry had found the tragedy almost too much to bear. He needed to escape, if only briefly, from the darkness of the trailer.

"I'm not unhappy with the song," said Joe. "It's got great potential, but it needs to be remixed."

Terry didn't agree. He liked it just the way it was. But Joe was adamant. It was going to be the first release on his new label and he couldn't risk failure.

"I'm thinking about getting Del Stuart to remix it," said Joe. "Do you know his work?"

Terry had heard of him, but he couldn't recall anything he'd done.

"Three top-five entries this year, so he knows what he's doing. He doesn't come cheap, mind you." Joe reached for his wallet. "That reminds me. Here." He handed Terry a fifty-pound note.

"What's this for?" asked Terry. "You've given me my train fares this week."

"Why don't you take young Maureen somewhere nice?" smiled Joe. "How is she, by the way?"

"All right, I think. I haven't seen her since the studio."

He began to feel guilty. He'd told her he'd see her after the funeral, but with things as they were, it was too difficult to leave the campsite. It had been bad enough trying to communicate with all those people he hardly knew (distant cousins and aunts, telling him how much he'd changed and what a pity it was that his father had never seen him looking so smart) without Belcher having to drop his bombshell. And then there was the drunken laughter. And the talk of chavvies and vardas and some words that Terry knew and many that he didn't. And the more they drank, the more obscure the language became and Terry couldn't understand what they were saying… and neither did he wish to.

Then the talk of Darenth Wood and the memories of the hop-fields. And they laughed when they should have been crying and they spoke of early days when they should've been thinking of his father, buried six feet under and unable to join the party.

And he and Billy had gone to sit by Abi's fire and stared into the flames, dreaming of how it *was*. But Belcher interrupted, sitting between them, cross-legged on the ground and they didn't want to hear what they'd guessed he was going to say.

"It was your dad's last wish that we moved on. He asked me to take the trailer up north. All of us. Up Leicester way."

Billy poked the fire with a stick and watched the sparks fly upwards. "I don't wanna go to Leicester!"

"There's more up there," said Belcher. "There's nothin' left down 'ere for your mother and not a lot for me."

So instead of going to see Maureen, Terry had stayed to comfort Billy. Though he should have phoned or sent a text. He *should* have… but he hadn't.

"She's a nice girl," said Joe.

"Yes."

"And she's very fond of you."

"I know."

Joe decided the time was right. "She was telling me about your background. Very interesting, Terry." He spoke kindly, trying not to make a big thing of it.

Terry was horrified. "She *what*?"

"She didn't realise I didn't know. Not that it matters, of course."

"She had no right!" said Terry. "It's got nothing to do with you!"

Joe put his hand on the boy's shoulder. "Don't be daft, Terry. It's got everything to do with me, even if it's just to protect you from the press. I mean, suppose you make it really big…"

Terry fell silent. He knew it would have had to have come out eventually and he didn't blame Maureen. She wouldn't have done it on purpose.

"And I've been thinking, Terry," said Joe. "It could be great publicity."

"No!" said Terry, firmly.

Joe tried to reason with him. "Terry, there's nothing wrong with being a gypsy."

"No! Definitely not!"

Joe crossed to the window and opened it. He stared at the wisteria, just creeping its way along the windowsill.

Terry approached him. "Look, Joe, if you use my family background for publicity, I'm off, do you understand? It's not *that* important to me!"

Joe turned to face him. "I thought it was everything to you, Terry."

"I'm warning you, Joe. I mean it!"

"All right. If that's what you want," grinned Joe. "If you don't want me to mention your family, then I won't. It's no big deal, son."

He opened his cocktail cabinet.

"What do you want?" he asked. "Coke?"

Terry waited at the school gates and watched as everyone left. There was no sign of Maureen. As he noticed Jim Buckley crossing the playground towards his car, he hastily looked around for somewhere to hide. But it was too late. The teacher had seen him and was approaching.

"Hello, stranger!" called Jim. "I can hardly believe it! You look so different!"

"Hello, Mr Buckley." Terry couldn't look him in the eye. "I'm waiting for Maureen."

"How's it all going then?" Jim seemed genuinely interested.

"Good."

"I was sorry to hear about your dad."

"Yeah."

"So... how's the record?"

Terry began to feel hot. "I'm sorry about what happened," he said. "It wasn't my fault. Honest. Joe didn't think your song was right for me. I didn't have any choice."

♪ 71 ♪

Jim smiled. "It doesn't matter, Terry. I'd have liked it to have happened of course, but, well…"

"I'll get you a copy of the CD as soon as it's ready," said Terry, adding quickly, "if you're interested, that is."

"Of course I'm interested, Terry," replied Jim. "And thanks. That'd be great."

Bob Jamieson placed his sports bag on top of Jim's car and yelled across the playground, "Are you going to give me this lift, or not, Mr Buckley?"

He'd seen Jim talking to a pupil and hadn't, at first, realised it was Terry Smith. When he recognised the boy, he strode over to them.

"Well, if it isn't the little pop star," he sneered.

Jim knew there could be trouble and tried to calm the situation.

"He looks good, doesn't he, Bob?" he said.

"Joe Fisher bought you all this lot, did he?" asked Bob Jamieson, eyeing the clothes.

"Yes." Terry was nervous. His old fear of Jamieson returned. Memories of cross-country runs and wall-bars, showers and towel flicking surged back. And the name-calling. Most importantly, the name-calling. And he was happy that school was behind him and that he'd never again have to face the changing room. But he couldn't understand why he was still afraid of this teacher who was no longer part of his life.

"How's your dad?" asked Bob. "Still in hospital, is he? Or has he gone to see your relatives in Australia?"

Jim was horrified. He knew that Bob couldn't have heard about it. Bob wasn't cruel, despite what Terry Smith thought.

"He's dead!" said Terry.

Bob was speechless. He looked at Jim for confirmation.

"Yes. Terrible, isn't it?"

"I'm so sorry," stammered Bob. "I didn't mean…"

"It's all right, Mr Jamieson," replied Terry. "Don't be embarrassed. It'll happen to all of us one day. Including you."

He began to walk towards the main staircase.

"I'll bring you a copy of my CD, Mr Buckley," he said. "I won't forget!"

Maureen was sitting in the cloakroom with her arm wrapped around Tracey, who was sobbing. Neither of them heard Terry approach.

"Oh, Tracey, don't," whispered Maureen. "It'll be all right. You'll forget him, you'll see."

Terry coughed.

When Maureen looked up and saw him standing there, she smiled and mouthed, "Won't be a minute."

She returned to comforting the almost hysterical Tracey with the clichés "There's plenty more fish in the sea, Trace" and "You're too good for him", while all the time she was thinking that she'd much rather be comforting Terry. They had so much to talk about. So much to catch up on. And here she was, giving solace to the redhead who she didn't really like.

Tracey eventually dried her eyes, which were beginning to match her red jumper, and slipped on her coat. She saw Terry and was startled.

"Don't worry about me," said Terry. "I'm just waiting for Maureen."

"It's Scotty," explained Maureen. "He's left school and he's told Tracey that he'll probably be too busy to see her for a while."

Tracey's face crumpled. "He's a pig," she whined. "I hate him." And the tears started to flow again.

"Has Scotty got a job then?" asked Terry as he and Maureen walked home to Gran's house.

Maureen realised that so much had happened in such a short space of time. She knew she had to tell Terry about Bury The Rabbit and their record and the interview on the radio. She decided she'd explain everything over a cup of tea at Gran's.

Sixteen

Mother understood, though Belcher didn't, why Terry wanted to go out for the night. She'd not have done the same when *she* was young, when *her* father had died. But times were different. She knew it wasn't for lack of feeling. She knew that Terry had cared deeply for his father.

"It's not been two weeks," said Belcher. "Ain't you got no respect?"

Terry didn't respond.

"You're still in mourning, you know," Belcher went on. "Anyways, where d'yous get the money from?"

"From Joe," replied Terry, guiltily, knowing that Belcher had paid for everything since his father had been taken ill.

"That's good, innit?" said Belcher, sarcastically. "I spend my money making sure yous get fed, while yous go and spend yours on nights out with your gorja girlfriend."

Terry pulled the fifty pounds from his pocket and held it out towards Belcher. "Here," he said. "Take it. It doesn't bother me. I'll stay in."

He meant it. It wasn't right. Why should Belcher have to pay for everything? Anyway, it only gave him more control over the family. More power.

Belcher looked at the money, then stared into Terry's eyes.

"Put it away!" he growled. "I don't need yer money. Your *mother* might, but..."

"No," Mother quickly interrupted. "No. I don't want it."

Terry slipped the money back into his pocket.

"You've got to sort yourself out, boy," went on Belcher. Terry detected the repressed anger in his voice. "And pretty quick too! This singing might be all right for some. Those that can afford to hang about doing nothing. But it ain't right for the likes of yous!"

Terry stared at his feet. The lecture was just like the ones Dad used to give. The "I'm a man of the world, son" type of lectures. "I'm older than you, therefore I *know*." Sweeping statements encompassing everything from joining the Euro to the truth about life after death, when in reality, God bless him, he knew nothing except this site, the price of a ton of lead and the licensing hours of The Three Stars.

And the voice of the man who used to take two hours to read a few pages of *The Sun*, trailing his index finger along each word as he mouthed the letters, trying to link them together, would get louder and angrier. Full of sound and fury, signifying nothing. Nothing that was of any value to Terry.

But still Terry loved him. And now he missed him. He missed him badly. And Belcher wasn't his father, nor could he ever hope to be.

"We'll be off soon," said Belcher. "I've told yous. We're going north. And you've got to decide if you're coming with us."

"I'm not," Terry replied, firmly.

"I can't support yous if I'm not here!" Belcher's voice was getting louder, sounding just like Dad's.

"I'll support myself," replied Terry. "If the record thing fails, there's lots of things I can do."

"You could always join us later on, Terry." His mother's voice was low and plaintive.

Terry went to her. "Oh, Mum. You know I can't," he said. "I'll come and visit. Often. But…"

"I know," she replied. "You're better off down here."

He wasn't sure, but he thought the tears were beginning anew in Mother's eyes. She'd cried so much since Dad had died and the rims of her eyes looked sore. So red. He knelt by her chair. He wanted to be alone with her. He wished that Belcher would go to his own trailer for a while. Just for a few minutes. But Belcher was practically living here now. And soon he'd sell his trailer and move in completely, taking over Terry's bed. Or his father's. He'd wondered about that before, but had dismissed the thought because he *had* to. He didn't want to believe *that*.

"D'you think Dad would've minded if I went out tonight, Mum?" asked Terry. "D'you think he would have cared?"

Terry's mother smiled at him. "He'd probably have told you to go and have a good time, son."

Belcher sneered and mumbled, just loud enough for Terry to hear, "You never went to see him when he was alive, so I shouldn't let him bother you *now*."

Terry kissed his mother on the cheek for the first time in years. He'd often wanted to but something had held him back. She didn't respond, physically. She didn't put an arm around him, or stroke his hair as she used to when he was a toddler.

"You're a good boy," was all she said.

For many years after, Terry would recall that one line, "You're a good boy."

To outsiders it may have sounded strange. To those families who touch and say what they feel, it could have been construed as cold. But Terry knew what she was trying to tell him. She loved him very much but, "You're a good boy" was the only way she could express it.

So with his mother's approval and with fifty pounds in his pocket, he and Maureen took the bus to the brighter lights of Greenwich, where they strolled along The Thames and where McDonald's fed them, giving them plenty of change.

Franco Rosetti had decided it was time to stop playing games and to get down to the real nitty-gritty. He'd invited Scotty and the Leroys, along with their parents, to discuss the future for Bury The Rabbit.

"Things are looking good," he declared, "but we've really got to decide where we're going. We've either got a group of school kids who play part-time in a band, or we've got a group of professional musicians with the ability to make a great deal of money."

He directed his comments at Mr and Mrs Leroy. "Ray and Phillip have left school, as you know," he said. "They want to concentrate totally on the future of the group. So I'm asking you to make a decision. We'd like the twins with us, of course, but if you feel they should stay on at school, then we'll have to replace them. I'm sorry, but that's the way it is."

Mr and Mrs Leroy weren't surprised. They'd been expecting this since the release of the record and had discussed its implications between themselves and the twins. Finally, they'd decided that it had to be the boys' decision... and naturally, Mark and John Leroy had accepted Franco's offer.

"Great!" enthused Franco. "Very sensible, lads!" He reached out and shook their hands. "Now... there's been a development in our favour," he informed them. "Robbie Jones from Viscount Radio has made some calls to a few people... and it looks as though 'Easy' will be going on to the BBC playlist."

"Hey!" yelled Rosetti. "Brilliant!"

"By the end of next week," continued Franco, "your record will have been heard by millions!"

Rosetti grinned at Scotty. "Top twenty, here we come!" He turned to his father. "Well done, Dad!"

"Cheers!" added Scotty.

"A glass of champagne, anyone?" asked Franco.

Seventeen

Maureen took the day off school to accompany Terry to the location of his pop video: a large, rambling house with extensive grounds near Surbiton. Vans, cars and cables were spilling over the lawns as Terry and Maureen arrived, half an hour late, with an apologetic taxi driver whose knowledge didn't include the wilds of Surrey.

Joe introduced Terry to the owner of the house, a tall, elegant woman in her mid-fifties who, with a smile, offered one hand, while the other held on to the collar of her over-zealous Red Setter.

Terry's co-star had already arrived. Suki was young, slim, blonde and, thought Terry, extraordinary beautiful. Maureen thought so too, and she felt a pang of jealousy when she noted that Terry couldn't take his eyes off her.

Coffee and bacon rolls were served in the unit bus, where Terry found his costume, labelled with his name and draped across a wire coat hanger.

"So, you're Terry," said Suki, sweetly. "Nice to meet you."

"You too," replied Terry. "This is Maureen."

Suki flashed a smile at Maureen. "Hi. Are you in the video too?"

"No," Maureen smiled back. "I'm just along for the ride."

"And for the bacon rolls, I bet?" giggled Suki.

Maureen laughed. "Yes, and the bacon rolls."

"Have you seen the storyboard, Terry?" asked Suki.

Terry nodded. "I didn't really understand it."

"Pop videos are always a bit like that," explained Suki, who'd appeared in dozens of them. "They're all very vague. But it's something to do with you being really poor and me being really rich."

Terry grinned. "So no acting needed there then."

Suki laughed, an infectious, high-pitched giggle, which set Maureen giggling along with her.

As the director and his crew continued to set up for the first shot, the costume supervisor entered the unit bus and handed Terry a large, golden earring.

"The director thinks this would be better than the one you're wearing, Terry," he said.

Terry took it from him. "It's huge!"

"It'll catch the light better," explained the costume supervisor. "Apparently." He shrugged. "But then what do *I* know. I just do as I'm told." He smiled and left, taking Suki and Maureen with him, allowing Terry some privacy as he changed into his costume: some ragged trousers, a collarless shirt, a flat cap and a pair of scuffed trainers.

Terry wandered from room to room of the large house, miming the words to 'Call On Me' as he stared open-mouthed at the pictures on the walls and ran his fingertips over the antique vases. Retake after retake showed him bewildered at his luxurious surroundings.

From the garden he then stared in at the drawing room, where Suki, elegantly dressed, sat at a desk, writing.

He mimed:

> "If you knew
> How much it hurts me
> To be left on the outside
> Looking in."

Through the window, she smiled coldly at the boy in ragged clothes, before approaching and drawing the curtains.

"A metaphor," explained the director, somewhat pretentiously, "He's being shut out of her life."

He was delighted at the way Terry responded to his direction. Seldom had he directed a pop singer with any acting ability and Terry's performance was all the more remarkable considering it was his first time before a camera. He called to his crew, enthusiastically. "That was very, *very* good. Right! Let's set up in the dining room for the last scene, gentleman and ladies!"

The flames from the huge, log-filled fireplace in the dining-room cast a flickering shadow across Terry's face, highlighting first the flat cap, pulled down over his eyes, then the collarless shirt... and finally the glint from the earring. Through the lens, Terry appeared as the stereotypical gypsy boy, sitting at his camp fire.

"That's magic, Terry," said the director. "Magic!"

He had just the picture he wanted.

Zodiac was one of the top promotion companies in London, handling every form of bankable face from top TV soap stars to the latest cartoon characters. Terry had come to the office knowing what to expect and, briefed beforehand by Joe, he knew what sort of questions he'd be asked. He'd arrived early and was placed in the smallest of the offices, which served as a waiting room, among piles of magazines and newspapers. He picked up a copy of *GO* and, checking the date, realised that it was today's copy and turned immediately, as he always did, to the pop charts. His eyes followed his finger as it slowly went down the page, indicating each of the top forty singles. Number twenty-five... no surprise. Number twenty-six... that one was surely destined for the top. Number twenty-seven. He stopped and stared. It couldn't be true. He read it again.

27- EASY – Bury The Rabbit (Sloop)

He was unable to hold the paper steady.

A woman appeared, in her mid-twenties, from the adjoining office.

"Terry Smith?"

"Yes," he croaked. He cleared his throat and tried again. "Yes."

She smiled. "Would you like to come through?"

He closed the paper and placed it back on the pile. Then he saw it. The front cover! He hadn't noticed it before. Why hadn't he seen it before? Rosetti's face, grinning up at him, filling the whole page. The headline screamed at him: 'EASY, RAY, EASY!' and in subtitles: "The Rosetti Interview."

Terry couldn't tear his eyes away from it. He kept staring... wanting to pick it up... wanting to read the article. And yet... *not* wanting to read it!

"Bury The Rabbit," said the woman, who'd noticed Terry's interest. "Have you heard them?"

"Yes," Terry almost stammered.

"Good record," she added, rubbing salt into gaping wounds.

"Yes."

"We're handling the merchandising," she said. "And we helped with the launch."

"Really?" was all Terry could muster.

"Got them moving pretty quickly too, I'm glad to say."

"Yes."

"It's because it had a good marketing line," she went on. "Schoolboy band and all that. Always better if we can find an angle which is a bit different."

Then came the bombshell.

"Their record plugger's trying to get them on to next week's *Chartbusters*."

"*Chartbusters*?" Terry hoped he'd misheard.

"I hope he manages it. They're nice lads," she grinned. "Especially Ray Rosetti. Absolutely charming."

Terry's head was swimming.

"Come on in," said the woman. "Let's see if we can find a good marketing angle for *you*."

Terry's pop video director had discovered the perfect location for his second day's shoot in New Cross. Among the rubble of a row of terraced houses, demolished to make way for a new upmarket development, his crew had built a huge bonfire. Old tyres and pieces of scrap metal were scattered across the site and water was poured everywhere before the ground was churned up by the wheels of the unit bus, to create piles of mud.

The film extras had arrived by coach, brought from their Central London pick-up point. They were clothed to look like the director's idea of yesteryear gypsies. All the women wore headscarves and long colourful skirts while the men wore flat caps, baggy trousers and torn shirts with rolled-up sleeves. There was an abundance of beads, earrings and red and white spotted neckerchiefs. Their hands and faces were dirtied with mud and they sat around the fire eating stew and mashed potato from tin plates. In the background, hired at great expense, was an authentic Romany wagon, complete with black and white horse.

Terry's stand-in was no older than thirteen; a handsome boy whose facial similarity to Terry was almost immaterial as only the back of his head and a glimpse of his profile would be filmed. Dressed in the costume which Terry had worn for the previous day's filming, he would sit, back to camera, staring into the fire. It was at this point that the director had planned to superimpose Suki's face. Then Terry, on seeing her image in the flames, would begin to dream. The dream sequence had already been filmed and had proved to be excellent.

As night fell, the director prepared his final shot: the Romany wagon disappearing from the site, watched by all the gypsies. From a distance, the stand-in, looking so much like Terry, peered back from the departing wagon at the beautiful girl who was trying to follow him, but was being dragged back by his gypsy family.

"Cut!" called the director. Then, "Well done, everyone! That's a wrap!"

"Well done, Suki," said Joe. "As beautiful as ever." He put his arm around her and she giggled. "You looked lovely in yesterday's rushes," he said. "It's going to be a great video."

"Thanks for the work, Joe," she replied, as she began to head for the bus.

"It should be good for you, you know," went on Joe. "If the record's a hit, it'll be shown quite a bit."

The director left the supervising of his crew and joined them. "Well?" he asked.

"Very good," said Joe. "I think."

"You only *think*?" The director laughed.

"I'll reserve judgement until I've seen the fully edited version."

"It's a pity Terry couldn't be here today," said Suki, innocently. "He'll love the finished thing."

Joe looked at the director and smiled.

They both watched as Suki climbed on to the unit bus.

"I'm not so sure about that," said Joe.

Eighteen

Terry wasn't expected. He'd arrived on the off chance that there'd be a few minutes to chat to Joe. He wanted to know if a date had been set for the release of the CD and he was also hoping to see the edited video.

"How about waiting in the office, Terry?" suggested Joe. "I won't be long."

Terry paced the office, pausing to gaze out of the window to the alleyway below. His mind was on Rosetti. If only Bury The Rabbit had released their CD after his own. If only he'd entered the charts before them. Then he panicked. Supposing 'Call On Me' didn't make it into the charts at all? He knew his record was better than Bury The Rabbit's! He could sing better than Rosetti and 'Call On Me' was a better song than 'Easy', but…

He ambled across to the desk and, without thinking, sat in Joe's chair. He looked around the room, noted Pete Shannon's gold discs, the limited edition cartoon prints, the designer wallpaper. His eyes flicked across the desk. Three telephones, a diary, a brown envelope marked TERRY SMITH. He was more than curious; he couldn't think what it could contain. The envelope wasn't sealed. He lifted the flap, gently slid his hand inside and gripped its contents. At first, he wasn't sure. He couldn't quite believe that the photos, picturing the boy with a tear rolling down his cheek, were of himself. There was his mother and Billy, their faces contorted with grief. And the other mourners. The coffin. The flowers. Terry's eyes began to mist. His chest was tightening, his breathing shallow and fast. His fingers trembled. Then he knew! These were for the tabloid newspapers; the gypsy boy pop singer at his father's funeral. He began to wonder about the video. The poor boy in the old ragged clothes. The dirty face. The large earring. Terry left the photos where they fell and slipped quietly from the office. He could still hear Joe's voice, talking to someone in the sitting room as he descended the stairs and staggered blindly into the mews.

Maureen wasn't at home. Gran had wheeled herself to the door and asked who was there. The knocking wasn't like Terry's usual knock, a gentle rat-a-tat-tat. This frantic banging had frightened her. She was always cautious about opening the door when she was alone, always called out to make sure she knew the caller. This time, when she heard Terry's voice, she was surprised.

"It's only me, Gran," he'd called back. "Is Mo there?"

"She's still at school, Terry," Gran had replied. She'd been about to open the door, knowing from the tone that something was wrong. Terry would make her a cup of tea and she'd listen to him.

But he'd called out, "I'll go to the school, Gran. I'll see you later!" and he'd gone.

Jim Buckley was surprised to see Terry standing at the classroom door.

"Maureen left five minutes ago, Terry," he smiled. "She said she had to get some shopping for her gran."

From the way Terry looked at him, Jim immediately knew that he wanted to talk.

"What's up?" he asked, seriously.

Terry sighed, almost groaning, "Sir!"

"Is it Maureen?"

"No. It's nothing like that." There was a slight tremble in the boy's voice. "It's Joe."

Jim saw that he was close to tears.

"He's got photos of my dad's funeral. He's going to use them, I think, for the papers."

"For the papers?"

"You know, for publicity. He wants people to know I'm a gypsy."

"Oh!" said Jim. "Come and sit down."

Terry crossed the room and sat in a vacant chair, bowing his head. Jim sat beside him.

"What am I going to do, sir?" he mumbled.

There was a long pause. Jim didn't know the answer.

"Does he know how you feel about it?" he asked, finally.

"Of course he does," said Terry. He looked up at Jim. his eyes filled with tears. "Why? Why does he have to do it? The record's good enough without all that."

"Perhaps he's thinking of *you*, Terry. He wants to make sure you're successful." The words were meaningless and Jim knew it. Joe's business depended on record sales and downloads and Terry was merely a commodity.

"I'd rather pack it all in than let him do that to my father," said Terry.

"Then do it," replied Jim, sharply. "Pack it all in, if that's what you really want."

"How *can* I?" Terry's voice rose. "The record's been made. So has the video. He can go ahead without me if he wants."

Jim smiled. "You know he can't go ahead without you. What about the interviews? The public appearances? Come on, Terry. You can't wait to be a star."

Terry glared at him. "I thought *you'd* understand."

"I do understand," said Jim. "I understand you want to be a successful pop singer. It's all you've ever wanted and nothing is going to stand in your way. You told me. You want to leave poverty behind you. You want to be rich and famous."

"But I don't want…"

Jim didn't let him finish. "But there's a price, Terry. There's a price to pay for everything you get out of this life and the sooner you realise that, the better."

Terry's temper began to flare. "I don't want my family background splashed all over the papers! I don't see why it should be. It's private. It's got nothing to do with my singing."

"It's the price of fame, Terry!" snapped Jim. "Get real, son! You know you can't have the sort of success you're aiming for without the public wanting to know details of your private life; what you had for breakfast, what sort of house you live in, who you're going out with! The public are hungry for it. And the tabloids feed them! It's big business, son. It sells papers!"

Jim walked back to his desk. He wanted to help, but there was nothing he could do.

"Mr Buckley!" Terry followed him, pleading. "What do I do, sir? Tell me what to do."

Jim spoke the words kindly. "You'll have to weigh up the odds, Terry. Then decide if it's all worth it!"

Terry was grateful for the lack of moonlight. It would make his job easier. He'd arrived at the mews just before three o'clock in the morning, quietly pushing his bike past the sleeping cottages, up the alleyway at the side of Joe's house. He leaned it against the wall and removed the old knapsack from the handlebar. As he slipped his arms through the strap, he looked up at the office window.

The house was in darkness and he hoped that Joe wasn't at home. If he were, he'd probably be in bed. And Terry, having seen the layout of the rooms, knew that the bedroom was on the floor above the office.

He'd done as Jim had suggested and concluded that the memory of his father meant far too much for him to allow it to be cheapened by Joe Fisher. He'd believed that his success as a singer was the most important thing in his life. He now knew differently. He couldn't sacrifice his family for fame and fortune. He wouldn't sell his soul for pop.

He used the wisteria to climb the wall, finding enough twisted branches for footholds, putting hand over hand to pull himself upwards, just as he'd been taught in the gym when rope climbing. Good old Jamieson! He laughed at the thought, almost out loud. The man had had a purpose in Terry's life after all!

He rested halfway and listened. There was silence; not even the distant hum of a passing car or a dog barking to be let in. The only sound came from his own heavy breathing and the thump, thump, thump of his heart.

He'd never done anything like this before. Others had. His father had. Others of his age who lived on the campsite had, but Terry always declined to join them, even when Billy had done it. This was the first time he'd ever stolen anything. And this wasn't really stealing. Or was it? No, it wasn't! He was only taking back what was rightly his!

As he climbed further, he wondered how he'd cope without Billy and his mother. There was no way he could go with them. It wasn't for the sake of his career, which had now finished before it had begun. He couldn't leave Maureen. Not now. She was the only person in the world who really understood him. There were no secrets with her.

He pictured the trailer setting off, Belcher driving, taking Mum and Billy to The Promised Land, which Terry was sure they'd never find. Jane at Berryfield was sad when she heard they were leaving. Mother had been there for years, since Billy was born. That's when they'd stopped travelling. Jane had watched the boy grow up. She'd seen Mother go through the good times and the bad, culminating in the death of poor Josh. Now their trailer would be replaced by somebody else's.

Terry tried the window, just in case. But it was locked as he'd expected, though why, he wondered, would anyone want to lock a window this far out of reach? He then began to worry that despite its inaccessibility, the window might be alarmed. He used the stone that he'd wrapped in his handkerchief to break the glass. One short, sharp crack. Then he waited and listened. On the first screech of an alarm or any slight sound which meant that Joe had been woken, he was ready to scuttle down the wall a lot faster than he'd climbed it. He waited and waited, but he heard nothing, so he slipped his sweating hand through the broken pane and released the catch. It was a tight squeeze, but he pulled himself through and tumbled, head first, on to the carpet.

Then a thought struck him. Perhaps 'Call On Me' wasn't there. Perhaps Joe had already passed everything on to Del Stuart. Maybe Del had already done the remix. His heart beat even faster. He groped around the darkened room until he touched the desk. He grappled for the switch and put on the lamp. Then he crossed to the filing cabinet and opened the drawer. There were some CDs, dozens of tapes from the video shoot and a small box with a handwritten label which read, 'For Del Stuart! Call On Me (Master Recording)…

Terry Smith'. There was even the envelope containing his photos. He slid the CDs, some of the tapes and the small box into his knapsack. He knew he should leave. Immediately. But there was one more job he wanted to do. He removed the photos from the envelope, tore each one in half and spread them across Joe's desk.

With his body now heavier with the video tapes, the CDs and the master recording of 'Call On Me', which had been destined to raise him to a bright new future, Terry began to worry that the climb down would prove difficult. But knowing that he had, with one defiant gesture, honoured the memory of the man he so loved, the descent to obscurity was easy.

Nineteen

Joe was furious. "What do you think I am? Some sort of monster?"

"The boy felt that the privacy of his family was being threatened," replied Jim. "What did you expect?"

Joe had woken early the following morning and was deeply shocked to find what Terry had done. He'd picked up the phone, intending to call the police, but had changed his mind and had rung Jim Buckley instead.

"It's Joe. I've got to see you."

"What's up?"

"Can we meet? It's about Terry."

"I'm teaching until four."

"Couldn't you get the morning off? It's urgent."

Jim wasn't sure what Terry had been up to. Perhaps he'd told Joe that he'd had enough; that he wanted out. But it was none of Jim's business and he had no intention of being a mediator.

"Please," said Joe. "I don't know where he is. I've rung that number at Berryfield but the woman won't tell me anything."

"I've got a job to do, Joe," said Jim.

"I don't want to call the police," Joe went on, "but if I don't find him, then I'll have to."

Jim couldn't imagine that Terry would do anything to warrant calling the police.

"The police? What for?"

"Can we meet?" Joe asked again.

Jim knew that he had a couple of free periods after registration and so offered to meet the man in his local café, The Greasy Spoon.

"There's a big florist's opposite," he said. "You can't miss it."

They ordered two teas and sat among the workmen who were eating their fried breakfasts.

"Where's this campsite, then?" asked Joe. "I'll strangle him, when I get hold of him."

"Hold on a minute," replied Jim. "I'm not telling you anything until you explain what he's done."

"He's broken into my office, that's what he's done!" Joe informed him. "He's taken loads of stuff including the master of his single. Probably thought that without it, we couldn't carry on."

"And you can?"

"Of course. I can get another one run off," said Joe. "It's all still on the studio's computer. But that's not the point!"

"So what *is* the point?" asked Jim. "What's your problem, Joe?"

"The point is, he's broken into my office, *intending* to steal the master recording of 'Call On Me'! The little idiot!" Joe was getting more heated. "I should never have taken him on. They're always the same, aren't they?"

Jim looked at him, blankly.

"Pikeys. They're all a bunch of thievin'…" he stopped himself, sighing deeply. "I should've known better."

"Hold on!" said Jim, angrily. "You were keen enough to use his gypsy background for your own ends, Joe!"

"I've invested a lot of money in that kid!" Joe fumed.

"He told me about the photos of the funeral," said Jim. "How could you even think about doing something like that?"

"He's good. He's a great singer. I could've made him a big star."

"But those photos? That's overstepping the mark, Joe."

"I had the photos taken before Terry said he didn't want to use his gypsy background as a publicity angle," Joe tried to explain. "When he was so adamant about it, I decided to destroy them. I just hadn't got round to it, that's all."

Jim couldn't tell if Joe was telling the truth.

"If he hadn't gone poking around, he'd never have known about it."

"So what do you intend to do now?"

"Talk to him, of course. Tell him that he's got it all wrong. That he's got *me* all wrong." There was a pathetic look in Joe's eyes as he spoke softly to Jim. "I'm not like that. Really, I'm not. That stuff you hear about unscrupulous pop managers exploiting their artists just to earn a quick buck is all rubbish. Storybook time!"

Jim was being convinced.

"I care about that kid, just as I've cared about Pete Shannon for the past thirty years. I wouldn't hurt Terry. Not for the world. I want success for that lad, Jim. I've had my share. Pete Shannon has made me a fortune. I don't need Terry Smith. He needs me. I could make him into something. I could make that boy a star!"

Jim swigged back the last of his tea and stood. "Come on," he said. "I'll show you where the campsite is."

Sylvie saw them first. Her eyes were sharp, and although the figures were still far away on the path which led to the campsite, she could tell by their gait that these were strangers approaching.

She called to Abi, who was throwing more branches on to his fire. "Gorjas, I think!"

Abi confronted them before they'd reached the camp. "Yeah?"

"We're looking for the Smiths," said Joe.

"Who wants them?" Abi's tone was threatening.

"We'd like a word with Terry," said Jim. "I used to be his teacher. I've been here before."

He hoped that that would make a difference. It didn't.

"He's not here," said Abi.

"Do you know where we could find him?" asked Jim.

"No idea." Abi was giving nothing away.

"Then could I have a word with his mother? She knows me."

"She's not here, either."

Joe decided to take up the conversation. He was getting impatient. "What time will she be back?"

"She won't," said Abi. He turned and started to walk away. "They've gone."

"Gone?" asked Jim. "Gone where?"

"No idea. Took the trailer off this morning." He walked slowly back along the path.

Joe whispered, "He's lying."

"I don't think so," replied Jim.

"Do you know where their caravan is?"

Jim led the way along the path. Abi looked back but said nothing, simply shrugged and walked over to his fire.

"It was just here."

Jim wasn't surprised. Where the Smiths' caravan had once stood, the grass was longer, greener.

Levi opened the door to his trailer and called out, gruffly, "If you're looking for them, forget it! They've gone up north!"

Abi poked at his fire with a long stick as he watched the two men disappearing into the distance. The fire crackled louder than usual.

"What you got on there?" asked Sylvie as she approached with a pot of potatoes.

"Just some rubbish that Terry gave me," replied Abi. He picked up the small box labelled 'Call On Me... Terry Smith' and threw it into the flames alongside Belcher's discarded belongings.

"I'd better get back," said Jim. "Double English this afternoon."

"Well, thanks for trying to help, anyway." Joe shook his hand. "If you get any indication as to where I can find him..."

"I'll let you know," interrupted Jim.

Jim had no intention of ever contacting Joe Fisher again. Terry had made his decision. He'd obviously gone north with his family and had given up the idea of becoming a pop singer. As far as Jim was concerned, the book was closed. And he felt a sense of admiration for young Terry Smith. He could have had it all. He could have been rich and famous, but he'd stuck to what he believed in. And that boded well for a kid just starting out in life.

"What about that Maureen?" asked Joe. "She goes to your school, doesn't she? Perhaps she'll know where he's gone."

"Maureen?" asked Jim. "Maureen who?"

"Doesn't matter," replied Joe. "See you around."

Maureen turned down the radio a little. Radio Viscount. She hardly ever listened to anything else nowadays.

"You should be at school, my girl," said Gran.

Terry opened the local paper. The back pages.

"I'll have to get a job pretty quick," he said. "I'm skint."

"You could always come back to school," suggested Maureen. "They'll let you."

"No way," replied Terry. "I'm not going back there. I hated it."

"It's not that easy to get a job, Terry," warned Gran.

"I'll be all right," said Terry. "If the worst comes to the worst, Levi says I can help him with the scrap. It's good money if you work hard."

Gran smiled. "I'm sure you'll be all right," she said as she wheeled herself towards the front room.

"I'm off," said Maureen. "Double English this afternoon." She slipped on her coat.

"You won't say nothing, will you?" It was silly to ask. Terry knew that she wouldn't.

"Of course I won't. As far as anyone's concerned, I don't know where you are."

"Thanks."

"I'll see you later then?" She began to leave.

"Maureen?"

She crossed to him and knelt by his chair. "Are you all right?" she asked.

"Have I done the right thing?" He gently placed his hand on the back of her neck.

"Of course you have," she assured him.

"Not that it really matters," he said. "I don't care about anything just so long as *you're* here."

"*I'm* here," she said. She ruffled his hair and smiled at him. "But I *shouldn't* be here. I should be at school."

Del Stuart started the run of Terry Smith's single. The voice which boomed from the speakers made the hairs on the back of Joe's plump neck tingle; a rarity for the man who'd been in the music business for decades.

Terry Smith sang:

> "You call on me
> When you are lonely
> And I know
> I can only
> Be a friend."

"Yeah. It sounds good, Del," said Joe. "Certainly better than the original mix."

"I think I can better it," Del replied. "I'd like to have the strings section rewritten. Can you give me until Monday night?"

"You do what you think best, Del," said Joe. "I can't argue with a genius."

"It's a surefire hit," Del assured him. "This Terry Smith's got an ace voice."

Joe snarled. "Yeah. I was going to use him to launch my new record label, but he's disappeared."

"Disappeared?"

"He didn't like the publicity we were going to use."

Del ran the song back to the beginning. "So what was this publicity then?"

Joe grinned. "He's a gypsy kid and we thought that that would be a tasty little morsel to dish to the tabloids. The silly little idiot didn't agree, did he? He didn't want his gypsy background mentioned. So he just went."

"He'll be back," said Del, confidently. "As soon as he hears his record's in the charts!"

Twenty

Levi carefully manoeuvred his beaten-up lorry along the narrow, potholed road which led to the back entrance of a row of shops.

"There!" Terry noticed two old fridges and a rusty cooker pushed against a large, yellow skip.

Levi leapt from the cab and made his way across the rubbish to the door marked 'Goods Entrance', where he rang the bell. Terry switched on the radio. It might be a long wait.

Levi earned a good living from his scrap metal business, though the wage he gave to Terry for helping him was only just enough for the lad to survive. Still, it was cash in hand. Tax free. And it stopped Terry from going on the dole.

The fitted-kitchen shops were the best. When new kitchens were put in, someone had to take away the old, used stoves and fridges, most of them in poor condition. Levi would offer to clear them away.

Terry had only been doing the work for a few weeks, since Belcher had taken the trailer north and Gran, to Maureen's delight, hadn't hesitated to give the lad a roof over his head.

"Just so long as you behave yourself with Maureen," she'd said.

Terry understood exactly what she meant. And Gran knew that Maureen wasn't a bit like that.

Today had been a very successful one for Levi and therefore an exhausting one for Terry. He wasn't exactly powerfully built and moving heavy pieces of metal all day was beginning to take its toll, especially on his back. He knew he couldn't stay in this job forever, but he had no idea what else he could do. He'd only ever had one ambition. To sing. To write songs. To make records. And now that was gone! For the time being, anyway.

Levi emerged from the back of the shop and nodded at Terry. He'd got permission to take the scrap.

"And this is number four in the Top Forty!" said the DJ. "'Easy'…
from Bury The Rabbit."

Ray Rosetti sang:

> "Got no intention of queuin' for the social
> Or windin' up servin' in a burger bar.
> I'd bust a gut before I'd give up losin'
> My faith in me… to make it as a star.
> And it's easy.
> Know what I mean?
> Easy!"

Easy for *some*! thought Terry. He switched off the radio, climbed down
from the cab and went to help Levi with the rust-covered cooker.

With Bury The Rabbit at number four in the charts, Sloop Records'
managing director was keen to talk to Franco.

"I suppose you want a release date on their follow-up, Franco?"
He moved across to his cocktail cabinet and took out a decanter of
whiskey and two cut-glass tumblers. "How's it going with Chas
Atkins, by the way?" he added. "Are the lads getting on okay with
him? He's a great producer. It's a wonder he was free to work with
them." He brought the whiskey and the glasses to his desk.

"They're getting on really well," replied Franco. "They've
recorded some great numbers for the album."

"Right! The album!" said the managing director. "Let's get
straight to the point, Franco. Have you thought about Ray doing
this album on his own?"

Franco was stunned. "How do you mean?"

"What if he went solo? How would that grab you? " He poured
two large whiskies from the decanter.

"But…" Franco grinned from ear to ear. "I don't believe I'm
hearing this."

"Let's suppose we remove Ray and replace him with another
lead singer?"

Franco gasped.

"So we get our album from Bury The Rabbit... *and* we get a solo performer. Ray Rosetti!"

"Are you serious?" asked Franco, amazed at the proposal.

"Very. I'm *very* serious, Franco. Look," he explained, "everyone here at Sloop Records thinks Ray's got a great future, *if* he's handled with care! With his looks, he's almost tailor-made for pop stardom. He stands out a mile from all those other young kids aiming for the charts at the moment. And if 'Easy' is anything to go by, he writes good songs."

"The others will never accept it," said Franco. "Scotty will go crazy!"

"Why? Scotty... and the rest of Bury The Rabbit will still have their record deal. What's he got to worry about?"

"But without Ray?" said Franco. "They'll never make it without Ray as their front man. You know that."

The managing director smiled. "That's not my problem, Franco. You're their manager. I'm sure you can sort that out."

"I'm gonna have to, aren't I?" Franco mumbled into his whiskey tumbler.

"But I suggest you don't let any of them know just yet, eh?"

"If you say so."

"Get me half a dozen *solo* Ray Rosetti tracks as soon as possible... just to reassure me, eh? Then we'll talk further." He raised his glass. "Cheers!"

Ray Rosetti flared. "It's *you*, Scotty! It's the drums! Get it together, will you?"

Scotty leapt from behind his drum kit and grabbed the front of Rosetti's shirt. Although tempers had been flaring all day, it was the first time in his life that Scotty had reacted in such a violent way towards his old school mate.

"*I* want it as right as *you* do, Ray!" he screamed. It's not just *your* future that's at stake, remember?"

The Leroy twins stood in front of their shared microphone, saying nothing, looking helplessly through the studio's glass panel towards their producer, Chas Atkins.

Chas had handled many temperamental artistes in his time and he was determined not to get worked up over two hot-headed teenagers.

Bury The Rabbit was recording 'Gimmee!', their second single for Sloop Records, and they'd personally chosen Chas Atkins as their producer. He had a list of hit CDs to his credit, including three number-one singles. Chas was expensive, but the boys were aware that having had a top-five single with their first release, they couldn't afford not to chart with their follow-up.

The boys were tired, having been up early for a photographic session for a German magazine. 'Easy' was due for release there the following week. Then they'd spent the day at KANSIT, Chas Atkins' new rehearsal and recording studio in Earls Court.

Chas had opened his studio just three months previously with his earnings from the Jam-On-Jam CD 'Get Up', which had topped the American Album Charts for months. As the money flowed in, Chas began to look for premises to build his dream: rehearsal studios to be hired out to top pop groups so that they could work in comfort… and with top security. At the moment, it was small-time, just two studios, but the huge Victorian building had the potential for at least six more units and Chas had great plans for the place: a restroom, canteen, offices etc. The word had begun to spread and in the past few weeks the studios had been booked solidly by some of the industry's top pop stars.

Chas had liked 'Easy' and he was in no doubt about the future success of 'Gimmee!' but he was surprised at just how good Bury The Rabbit's songs were. He was also surprised at Ray Rosetti's input, which was almost nil. It was, he realised, Scotty who was the real talent behind the group. It was Scotty who had most of the ideas. It was Scotty who wrote almost all of the lyrics and came up with the catchy guitar riffs. He only allowed Ray Rosetti to change the odd line, here and there. In public, Bury The Rabbit was Ray Rosetti's group. In reality, it was all controlled by Scotty.

Chas laughed to himself. He'd seldom come across any young pop singer who was as arrogant as Rosetti and yet, apart from his incredibly dark and handsome looks, the boy had very little to offer.

"Okay, lads. That's enough," said Chas, through the talkback system. "Time's money. We'll do the drum break again, Scotty. The rest of you can come in here."

Scotty glared at Ray Rosetti and climbed back behind his drums. Ray and the Leroys went into the control room and sat either side of the loudspeakers.

Franco entered and, noting that the boys had broken, he asked Chas if he could talk to them for a few minutes.

Scotty joined them.

"What do you want first, boys?" grinned Franco. "The good news or the brilliant news?"

"Let's have the brilliant news first eh, Dad?" laughed Rosetti.

"I think I may have convinced Sloop Records that you're ready to make your first album!" he explained.

"Fantastic!" yelled Scotty.

He smiled at Ray, who smiled back at him. For a moment, their quarrel was forgotten.

"And now...!" Franco announced, dramatically. "Here's the *good* news. How about... you've just been booked for your second *Chartbusters'* appearance?!"

"Great!" said the young Rosetti. "Brilliant! Number one, here we come!"

As the session ended, Franco led Ray to an adjoining office. "I want a word, son. Privately."

Scotty and the Leroys were convinced that Chas Atkins had had a word in Franco's ear about Ray's behaviour. They were wrong.

"As you know," said Franco, in a hushed voice, " I've been at Sloop Records all day today."

"Yeah."

"There's been a development."

"Yeah?"

"It's a very *big* development, Ray!"

Ray Rosetti gulped, fearing there was now some bad news to come. "Go on."

"They want to replace you with a new lead singer. They want you out of the group, son."

Ray Rosetti's face whitened. "What? Why the...?"

"Don't panic!" interrupted his father. "It's better than you think. They've decided they want an album from *you*! Solo!"

Ray Rosetti gazed open-mouthed at his father. He wasn't sure if he'd heard correctly. "Are you kidding me?"

"Now, why would I do that?" laughed Franco. "They want to hear some tracks from you before they conclude the deal, but that's no problem. Everyone at Sloop Records thinks you can do it on your own. To tell you the truth, none of them believe that Bury The Rabbit will survive the year... even with a new lead singer. Sloop's managing director was saying he doesn't like the group's image; he thinks they all fade into the background when you're on stage."

"I'm glad he thinks that," sneered Rosetti. "I've always thought that. As far as I'm concerned, Bury The Rabbit is just Ray Rosetti's backing group!"

"Not any longer," smiled Franco. "Sloop Records aims to build you into a big star, son. Everyone thinks you can do it. And so do I!"

"I *know* I can do it, Dad!" beamed Ray Rosetti. "When are you going to tell Scotty and the Leroys?"

"Not today," replied Franco. "I've got to think how to do this. Monday. I'll break it to them on Monday!"

Twenty-one

Chas Atkins knew nothing about the impending split of Bury The Rabbit and he found Rosetti's mood strange, to say the least. Rosetti had appointed himself as the spokesman for the group and would usually spend much of the recording session telling the producer how to do his job. Today he was quiet. Chas put it down to the fact that the boy was satisfied with the new single, which was almost finished.

Franco sat silently at the back of the control room, sipping coffee as he aimlessly flicked through a copy of *Music Forum*.

"Right, boys. That's it!" said Chas. "Come on in and listen."

As the group entered the control-room to listen to a rough-mix playback of 'Gimmee!', Ray Rosetti looked across at his father and gave a half smile. He wasn't looking forward to Scotty's reaction this morning!

Chas started the recording and Rosetti's voice, sounding more powerful than it had ever done, screamed from the speakers:

> "I took the warning
> Like a storm in a teacup.
> What d'you want me to do
> If your world is warmin' up?
> We're goin' out soon
> So I'll live it up while
> I'm still in credit.
> I'm goin' in style!"

Scotty thumped Rosetti on the back. "You sound fantastic, mate!" he said.

Rosetti stared straight ahead, saying nothing.

John and Mark Leroy grinned contentedly.

Chas Atkins faded the song as he turned to face the group. "Well?" he asked.

"Great, Chas!" said Franco. "Even better than 'Easy'. It can't fail."

Scotty opened his mouth to speak and Franco held up a hand to silence him. "I'd like a word with you, Scotty," he said, seriously. "And with you, John and Mark."

They could tell by the tone of Franco's voice that all was not well.

Ray Rosetti started to tremble. "I, um… I'll just go and get us some coffee," he said.

Scotty exploded. "You can't do that! We've been working for six months solid on this group. We've just gone to number two in the charts! You just can't do it!"

"I'm sorry, Scotty," replied Franco. "But we can. If you look carefully at your contract with me, and then at your contract with Sloop Records, you'll see. We *can* do it, son!"

"He doesn't mean legally!" added a fuming John Leroy. "We know you can do it legally. But morally? How can you, after all this time, just tear everything apart? We've worked hard for this success…"

"And how do you think Ray will cope on his own?" interrupted Scotty. "I wrote seventy-five percent of 'Easy'. And nearly all of 'Gimmee!' Ray's not a songwriter and you know it!"

Ray Rosetti appeared at the door with a tray of coffee. "That's all *you* know!" he said.

Scotty glared across at him. "You creep!"

"Now, come on, lads," Franco said, quickly. "Let's not get into a slanging match."

Chas Atkins took a coffee from Rosetti's tray and left the control room without speaking.

"I suppose *he* knew all about this too, did he?" snapped Mark Leroy.

"No," replied Franco. "This is the first Chas has heard about it."

"So…!" said Scotty. "What happens to 'Gimmee!'?"

Franco kept his voice low, trying to calm the boys. "It'll be released as soon as 'Easy' is out of the top forty."

"As Bury The Rabbit or under the name of Ray Rosetti?" sneered John Leroy.

Ray Rosetti looked at his father nervously. What would be the reaction to *this* bombshell?

"As 'Bury The Rabbit featuring ROSETTI'," he said.

"No!" screamed Scotty. "No! No! No!"

There was a brief silence, broken calmly by Mark Leroy. "No way. You can count me out."

"Me too," added his twin. "I'm having nothing to do with it."

Franco's face reddened with anger. "You'll all do exactly as I say!" he shouted. "I own this group and I'll manage it in whatever way I see fit!"

Scotty approached him and looked closely into Franco's eyes. "You don't own *me*, Mr Rosetti! Nobody owns me! You go ahead and release the new single in any way you like. But I won't be there to promote it! As from now, I quit!"

"Me too," added Mark Leroy.

John Leroy nodded his agreement.

"I'll sue!" threatened Franco.

"So sue!" Scotty responded.

He left the control room, followed by the Leroys.

Franco grinned across at his son. "That wasn't 'Easy', Ray."

Ray Rosetti smiled encouragingly. "Had to be done, Dad."

"And I suppose it's even better than I'd hoped for," added Franco. "At least we don't have to worry about the future of Bury The Rabbit. They no longer exist."

"One-hit-wonders!" laughed Rosetti.

Ray Rosetti's mother knocked on the bathroom door.

"Ray?"

"I'm in the shower, Mum," he called. "Did you get it?"

Mrs Rosetti opened *The Sun* and folded back the appropriate page.

"Yes," she said.

"And?"

"It's all right."

"Front page?" he asked.

He opened the bathroom door, still dripping wet, with a towel tied around his waist.

"No. Not quite."

He made a grab for the paper but she pulled it from him.

"You dry yourself first," she said. "You're dripping water all over the carpet."

She turned her back on him and began to head up the next flight of stairs to his bedroom. "I'll put it on your bed."

He tore past her, snatched the paper, leapt up the stairs and hurried into his room, closing the door behind him.

"Raymond!" she shouted. "Don't you sit on your bed in that wet towel."

He sat on the bed and read the article, headlined:

BURY THE RABBIT BREAK UP... EXCLUSIVE

And he liked what he read. Rica Stubbs, bless her, had written exactly what she said she would. She'd promised to show him in a good light... and she'd kept her word. Scotty and the Leroys came across as just hangers-on with no talent, although she'd been very careful not to use those exact words.

He'd met up again with Rica, two days after his group had split, and having discovered that, as well as her work at GO magazine, she also worked as a freelance journalist, he immediately suggested that she might write a piece for *The Sun*. He knew Rica liked him. She'd do anything he wanted. She found him incredibly attractive. But then didn't most girls?

He stood and looked at his still wet body in the full-length mirror. He wasn't surprised that he'd got all those girls in the *Chartbusters'* audience screaming for him. The body was perfect. No gym. No weight-training. All natural. He ran his hands over his firm, smooth-skinned chest, nicely tanned from regular use of his mother's sunbed – and smiled, checking the brilliant-white teeth as he did so. He squeezed a little gel on to his fingers and ran them through his already shiny, jet-black hair. Everyone fancied him. He knew that. He was beautiful. Even pretty little Maureen couldn't resist him. Maureen. He was thinking about her again. Why couldn't he get her out of his head? Hadn't she dumped him for that gypsy? Smith! Terry Smith! How Rosetti hated him. Nobody had ever dumped Ray Rosetti. Nobody except Maureen. His heart began to beat faster. Maureen. The only girl he'd ever really wanted. She could have had it all if she'd stayed with him: money, nice clothes, fun times…

And he wondered… what if he called on her? Perhaps if he just turned up one day when Smithy the Gyppo wasn't around…he wondered… he wondered if she…?

Scotty arrived at the restaurant just before one o'clock to find Chas Atkins waiting for him at the bar.

"Drink?" asked Chas.

"Just some orange juice," replied Scotty.

Chas ordered, as Scotty looked around at the diners: a host of famous faces from the worlds of TV and pop.

"So, what's this all about, Chas?" he asked. "Why did you want to see me?"

"Give me five minutes before I explain," replied Chas, with a broad smile. "I'm expecting someone else to join us."

"I'm here," said a voice from behind them.

"Sam!" laughed Chas. He shook the newcomer's hand.

Scotty stared at the tall, good-looking man who pulled up a bar-stool and sat between them. He'd seen him before, but he couldn't place where. He was in his forties, at least, with strikingly handsome features: very long, blond, almost white hair and brilliant blue eyes.

"Scotty, this is Sam," said Chas. "But *you* – and the whole world – probably know him as 'Bif'."

Scotty gasped. Bif from The Thunderdomes, one of the greatest rock bands of all time. He looked so different in a suit.

"I didn't recognise you at first," said Scotty. Sorry." Then he added, "I think you're great. One of the best drummers around."

"And this is Scotty," said Chas, finishing his introductions.

"*Was* one of the best drummers around," corrected Bif, with a grin. "We haven't done anything for two years."

Scotty couldn't believe it was that long. He was sure he'd been in the charts recently.

"What about 'Coming On Cold'?" asked Scotty. That was top-forty last year, wasn't it?"

Bif laughed. "A re-issue of an old song, probably recorded before you were born. They used it for a TV commercial... and it caught the public's attention."

"Bif's looking to invest some of his millions in KANSIT, my recording studio," explained Chas.

"Well, a few hundred thousand anyway," Bif interjected, winking at Scotty.

"We're aiming to expand the business in a big way," said Chas. "You've seen the premises, Scotty. It's gonna be fantastic."

"The builders are working on it right now," enthused Bif. "KANSIT will be the best studio complex in London by the time we've finished. There isn't an artist in the business, solo performer or pop group, that won't be using it by the end of the year. We're determined that it's going to be mega-successful."

"And from there, as a sideline, we're also going to run our own production company," explained Chas. "And form our own record label."

Scotty looked from Bif to Chas Atkins and back again.

"Hold on," he said. "Why am *I* here? What's this got to do with me?"

Bif grabbed his arm. "I've heard your stuff, Scotty," he said. "'Easy' is a great song. Really commercial. And I happen to think that 'Gimmee!' is even better."

Chas looked across at Scotty, guiltily. "Sorry, Scotty," he said. "I ran off a copy so that he could hear it."

"You can really write songs, man!" said Bif.

"Thanks," replied Scotty. "But you're forgetting something. I wrote those songs with Ray Rosetti."

"Rubbish!" laughed Chas Atkins. "I know how much Rosetti

put into those numbers. I've watched you working, don't forget." He paused. "Why on earth did you let him take all that credit?"

"His father held the purse strings, didn't he?" said Scotty. "Without Rosetti there wouldn't have been a group."

Chas looked at Bif. "I told you!"

"Well?" asked Bif.

"Well what?" said Scotty.

"How about joining us?" proposed Chas. "You and I can write and produce the songs and Bif can see to the business side."

Scotty was stunned.

"Could make you a very rich man, Scotty," grinned Bif.

"I… I don't know," replied Scotty. "I don't know if I'm *that* good a songwriter… and I know nothing about production."

"You're a great songwriter, man! Great!" argued Bif.

"And I can teach you all there is to know about producing hit records," added Chas. "Nothing to it!" he laughed.

"I'll have to think about it," stammered Scotty. "This is all a bit sudden."

"Don't take too long, man," smiled Bif. "You're at the top of a very long list."

"When do I have to decide?" Scotty asked, knowing that he was interested in the idea, but not sure if he wanted to give up his performing career for a life in the studio."

"How about giving us a call tomorrow?" suggested Bif. "Sleep on it."

Twenty-two

It had been one of the worst Sundays Maureen had had in ages. She'd done the usual chores – getting Gran's papers, doing her French homework, cooking the roast etc – but all this without Terry by her side to make light of it. She missed him so much. Saturdays and Sundays were the days that she always used to look forward to. But not lately. Terry was working away so much nowadays. Every weekend he and Levi went to collect scrap from as far as Lincoln and Norfolk. They'd started to stay away for two or three nights at a time, bedding down as best they could in the cab of the lorry. And for how many weeks was this going to go on? Maureen couldn't bear it if it was always going to be like this.

As Gran dozed in her chair, half-listening to the hymn singing on the TV, Maureen took the radio through into the back room. She and Terry always did this on Sunday afternoons, when he was at home. They never missed the Top Forty. And today, after that splurge of publicity about the split between Rosetti and Scotty, she was sure that Bury The Rabbit would climb that one place to the important number one slot. With that in mind, perhaps it was best that Terry *wasn't* here. She hated seeing that look on his face whenever Rosetti made new ground in the charts. Number two had been bad enough, but...

Maureen had been unusually irritated by Gran, who'd woken just as the countdown had reached the top five, calling out, "Mo, love! Make us a nice cup o' tea. There's a good girl."

So she'd carried the radio with her into the kitchen to wait for the kettle to boil, just in case the group had dropped to number three or four... though she very much doubted it.

She'd managed to deliver the tea and return to the back room just in time to hear the number two record. A non-mover! 'Easy' from Bury The Rabbit. So they hadn't made it. Not this week, at least.

There was a knock on the front door and Maureen's heart suddenly skipped a beat. For a fleeting moment she wondered if Terry had got home earlier than expected, but then, remembering he had his own key, she switched off the radio and made her way along the hall.

"Someone at the door, Mo!" called Gran.

"It's all right, Gran!" she called back. "I'm here."

The visitor knocked again, louder this time.

"I'm coming!" said Maureen.

She opened the door.

And she stared.

"Well, well, well," she smiled. "Hello stranger."

"Who is it, Mo?" shouted Gran.

"Can I come in?" he asked.

Having spent two weeks at number two in the charts, 'Easy' dropped like a stone; twenty-six, thirty-nine… and out! Franco and Ray Rosetti had hoped that it wouldn't disappear quite so quickly. It wouldn't have been so bad had there been a follow-up single ready for release, but both father and son agreed that 'Gimmee!' should be forgotten.

The upper floors of KANSIT were still under construction, although the basement and ground floors were ready: three recording studios, four rehearsal rooms and a half-functioning canteen. Franco, having no idea that Scotty had joined forces with Chas Atkins, hired the smallest of the rehearsal rooms so that his son could work with a group of session musicians. Most of the album had been written, but expert musicianship was needed to hone and polish the songs before taking them into the recording studio.

All of the musicians loathed the supercilious young pop singer, who would scream abuse at them if he felt they were slacking in any way, but every one of them agreed that the songs were good, and with the right producer, Ray Rosetti had a massive hit on his hands.

"He's gonna be a big star, that's for sure," said the drummer.

"Without doubt," agreed the keyboard player. "Mores the pity. The arrogant little yob!"

Terry took the coach to Leicester. It was cheaper than the train. Maureen had wanted to take a couple of days off school to go with him, but they couldn't afford the two fares. He gazed out of the window at the passing scenery and cursed at the thought that these two treasured days off, which Levi had given him, had to be wasted on travelling north.

Billy had come down to their old campsite, Berryfield, a few weeks previously and informed Levi that Mother was getting married again, and he'd asked if Terry would be able to make it to the wedding? Terry wouldn't.

"You mustn't be like that, Terry," Gran had said. "She needs a bit of happiness, does your mother. Look at what she's been through. Don't begrudge her a bit of happiness, love."

But he did. He couldn't help it. He begrudged her *that* sort of happiness. It was too early. Disrespectful and far, far too early.

Belcher met him at the coach station. The huge bear of a man flung open the door to his van and yelled out, "So you've made it, then?"

Terry hauled himself into the cab, and the two drove along in silence until they reached Lowes Farm. Belcher had obviously wanted to speak. Terry hadn't.

"See?" said Belcher, as they bounced down the dirt track towards the dozen or so trailers. "Better than Berryfield, innit?"

It wasn't better. It was much worse. More mud. More scrap metal. More dogs running around than Berryfield had ever had. And two tethered ponies looking, Terry thought, rather undernourished. He wondered if he was being unfair. Perhaps his mind had been clouded by the thought of his mother actually marrying this man whom he'd never liked: Belcher.

Mother was waiting, nervously, on the trailer steps, aware of what Terry would be thinking. She hoped he wouldn't react as aggressively as young Billy had. At least he'd come all the way to Leicester to see her and she hoped it was to wish her well. The wedding was to take place the following Saturday and it was a pity that he wouldn't be able to come to the ceremony. All the family and many of their friends had said they'd make it, even Uncle Render, who was right up in Scotland now. It was a pity Terry couldn't be there. But she understood. And at least he'd taken the trouble to phone and say that he was coming up this Monday. She hoped he was going to be kind. She didn't want any more aggression.

"Oh, Terry," she said. "Thank you for coming, boy."

On the journey, he'd planned what he was going to say. "My father's lying six feet under… hardly cold… in a grave which you've conveniently deserted… to come and live up here, with your boyfriend… and now that you've decided to marry him, supposing you tell me the truth, eh? That you two have been planning this for ages, even while my father lay dying in hospital!"

But he didn't say any of these things. He squeezed her tightly and sighed, "Mum. Oh, Mum."

Terry and Billy walked across the field towards the campsite. Terry had needed this time to be alone with his brother, to find out how he truly felt. The night before, after tea, they'd all sat and talked about the old times, just like they were a real family, except of course they *weren't* a real family… and could never be. Not without Dad.

Terry had to set off for the coach station within the next hour or so and he felt no sadness at leaving although, curiously, the thought of feeling no sadness at leaving his family *did* sadden him. A little. This place had never been his home. Even Berryfield was no longer his home. His home was now with Maureen and Gran. That's where he felt he really belonged.

"How's the new school?" he asked Billy.

"Same as the old one," replied Billy. "I hate it!"

"No friends?"

"Only me mates from here. From the campsite." He paused. "I hate gorjas," he said, finally.

Terry put an arm around his brother's neck affectionately, as he always used to. "You don't, Billy," he said. "Don't be daft. Not all of them."

"Gorjas hate *us*," said Billy, "so why can't we hate them back?"

"You don't hate Maureen, do you?" asked Terry. "She's a gorja. You don't hate her."

"I wouldn't rob her," replied Billy.

Terry waited for him to explain this strange statement. He didn't.

"I ain't stayin' here, you know, Terry?" Billy suddenly blurted out. "I ain't stayin' here. Not with 'im and 'er!"

"You have to, Billy," sighed Terry. "Where else are you gonna go?"

"Dunno, yet!"

"Mum would be ever so upset if you ran away," he added. "She really cares, you know."

Billy sneered at the comment. "Oh yeah? Then why's she marryin' 'im, when she knows I hate 'im?"

"Billy..." he pleaded. He remembered Gran's words. "She needs a bit of happiness. Look what she's had to put up with. Don't begrudge her that, Billy. Please."

They walked on in silence for a while.

"You shouldn't have given up that pop star thing," said Billy, suddenly.

"You know why I did it." Terry thought that he'd explained all this once.

"Yeah. You did it for the family. You told me. Because you didn't want to hurt them."

"That's right."

"*They* don't mind about hurting people though, do they?"

"Don't be daft."

"It's true!" Billy's voice was getting louder. "You cared about *her* and now she's gonna marry Belcher, no matter what *you* think about it! And you cared about Dad... and he went and died, Terry. And you cared about me! And I wanted you to be a pop star. So why did you do it, eh? Why did you do it, Terry? It was the only thing I was looking forward to. My brother doing somefink. And now you're doing nuffink! Just like I'll do nuffink." He burst into tears. "Just like Dad did nuffink." He covered his eyes with his sleeve and sobbed. "Why d'you do it, Terry?"

Twenty-three

Del Stuart used Triumphant Studios to finish the remix of Terry Smith's song. He worked late into the night, until he and Joe were pleased with the result:

'Call on me
You'll find a stranger.
I gotta change,
It's not the same anymore...'

"That's it, Joe," beamed Del. "A smash hit!"

Joe sighed. "I could've made that boy a star. I wonder what the silly little idiot's doing for a living now?"

"Laying tarmac, probably," replied Del. "That's what they all do, don't they, gypsies?"

Joe's new record label, Fat Tracks, was ready to be launched and 'Call On Me', whether Terry Smith liked it or not, was going to be its first release.

Terry and Levi arrived back late from Norwich, where they'd been working, and having said their goodnights Terry leapt on his bike and headed home. Maureen wouldn't be expecting him as he'd sent a text to say that they were sleeping overnight in the cab of the lorry. Then, Levi had changed his mind.

"If I put my foot down, we can be back at Berryfield before eleven," he'd said.

Gran's house was, as he'd expected, in total darkness. He slipped his key into the lock and opened the door very quietly. He knew he mustn't wake Gran, as she would panic, thinking that someone had broken in. He heard her snoring loudly and knew that she hadn't stirred, so he wheeled his bike into the hall, parked it against the wall and grabbed the handrail. He crept up the stairs, past Maureen's closed door and into his bedroom, where he undressed without turning on the light, and climbed into bed feeling… content. Feeling at home.

He was just dropping off to sleep when he realised he needed to go to the bathroom. He climbed out of bed and, with his eyes now accustomed to the dark, he made his way along the landing. Suddenly, the whole area was lit by car headlamps. He crossed to the window and looked down into the street. It was a taxi. Two people got out: a young man and a girl.

"No!" said Terry. "Oh, no! " He turned away from the window, feeling sick. It couldn't be true. It couldn't! Not Maureen. Not Maureen and him. Not him! Not Rosetti!

When Terry returned to Berryfield it was well past midnight. The dirt path to the campsite was unlit and, as there was no moon that night, he groped his way around until he came to Levi's trailer. He hoped, as he wheeled his bike into one of the many washing-line supports, that he hadn't woken Abi's dog. It would be no good trying to explain to that ferocious mongrel that he wasn't a gavver; that he was, in fact, one of their own. The beast would have his neck in its jaws before he had a chance to cry out.

The journey on the bike from Maureen's, carrying his holdall of meagre possessions, was arduous but he knew that he had to get away immediately. Finding Levi's trailer, he tapped lightly on the door and waited.

"Who is it?" a voice called.

"It's me, Levi," Terry replied. "Can I bed down here?"

Levi turned on the lights and opened the door.

"What happened?" he asked. "Lost the key to your girlfriend's house?"

"No," Terry replied. "Worse."

"Then you'd better come in, hadn't you?" yawned Levi. "But don't bring that bike in with you."

Terry couldn't sleep. Levi had only one bed so he'd spread a few coats across the sofa.

"It'll have to do," he said. "I ain't a guest house."

The thin, wooden slats beneath the cushions dug deeply into Terry's back and he knew that he wouldn't be able to stand this for more than a couple of nights, though he had no idea where he'd move to. There was no way he'd go back to Gran's. He would never, ever go back there. Not back to Maureen. Not to her. Not after what she'd just done. Had it been any other guy in the world that he'd seen her with, he might, just *might* be able to forgive her. But with him? With Rosetti? There was no way he'd ever forgive her for that!

Rosetti's solo single, 'Down On Me Gently', had a low-key launch. Rosetti was clever at interviews; he was always humble, forever talking about his working-class origins and how his parents had sacrificed everything to give him a chance in life. The record was selling in modest quantities by the time it appeared on the BBC playlist and from then on, the sales figures shot up.

The video was simple; no exotic locations. Rosetti, dressed as a schoolboy, his tie loosened and his shirt collar undone, sat at a desk, gazing lovingly across a mist-filled classroom, towards a beautiful model.

He sang, romantically:

"All I need is the opportunity
To tell you what you really mean to me
But if you feel the need to put me down…
Then put me down gently.

If, when you're within my arms, you find
You don't relax within these arms of mine
And you feel you have to put me down…
Come down on me gently."

And as the video was shown on Saturday morning TV, thousands of girls throughout Britain began to fantasise about the schoolboy Rosetti. Somehow, dressed like this, dressed as one of their own, he became more attainable. And they thought about the Peters and Matthews and Davids in their own classrooms and they wondered why they didn't have a handsome, half-Italian lad like Rosetti to get them through double maths.

Yes, the girls loved him. And the boys hated him. And as they watched, a flood of memories came back for others, those who'd actually shared a classroom with him: Scotty... and Terry... and Maureen!

Jim Buckley gave out the marked English books. He'd been pleased with most of the essays and felt that many of his class would eventually achieve good results, though he still regretted that his best pupil, Terry Smith, had left school in order to pursue a career in pop music. Terry wasn't the only one he'd lost... though he was only too pleased when Ray Rosetti had left for exactly the same reason. Unfortunately, Rosetti was achieving his goal. Terry Smith had lost it all; thrown it all away.

"Maureen," he called, as the lunchtime pips sounded, sending his pupils rushing from the classroom. "Can I have a word?"

She approached his desk, a little shamefaced.

"I know what you're going to say, sir," she said. "I know it was awful. I'm sorry."

"It was the worst piece of work you've ever given me, Maureen," he affirmed. "What's up? You've always been one of the best in the class."

She didn't hesitate; she was grateful she could talk to someone she trusted. "It's Terry."

"Terry? What's the problem? He's all right, isn't he?" Jim sounded concerned.

"I don't know, sir," she replied. "I haven't seen him for weeks."

Jim was surprised.

"I've done something really silly, Mr Buckley," she said. And she poured out her heart.

Joe Fisher invited Del Stuart to his luxury office-cum-home, so that they could watch the pop video on, as Joe put it, "the big screen".

The video, depicting Terry Smith as a gypsy being rejected by a beautiful aristocratic young girl, had, Del thought, great style.

"To be honest, Joe," he said, "I thought 'Call On Me' was a top-five hit. I'm now convinced it's a number one. That video is superb."

"I thought so too," replied Joe. "A lot of editing was needed 'cause he stole some of the tapes, but that finished cut is fantastic, eh? Can you now see why I'm desperate to get that kid back? He's got the makings of a great star."

"You don't have an address or anything, then?" asked Del.

"No." He sighed. "Just the address of a gypsy site in Kent. I went there, but the whole family had moved on. Taken their caravan up north somewhere."

"And no one could tell you where exactly?"

"Oh, I'm sure they could. If they wanted." He laughed. "Gyppos!" he went on. "They're such a tight-knit lot, you know. Won't let anyone into their circle unless they're absolutely sure about them."

"I'm sure they can be bought," sneered Del. "You know what pikeys are like. Give them enough money and they'll soon forget all that loyalty stuff."

Joe was all ears. "Do you think so?"

"I know so!" replied Del. "They'd sell their own grandmothers for twenty quid."

"Perhaps I should pay Berryfield another visit," pondered Joe. "And this time take a few tenners in my pocket."

"*I* would," said Del. "What can you lose?" He grinned. "Apart from your front teeth?"

Both men laughed.

"Watcha gonna do then?" The voice made Terry jump. It was almost three in the morning and Levi had got out of bed to come to talk to him.

"Do you want a cuppa?" asked Levi. "I can't sleep."

"Me neither," said Terry.

Levi tutted. "I'm not surprised. You must be so uncomfortable using that old sofa as a bed. It's had its day."

Terry looked up at him and smiled.

"You can't stay there forever, Terry," he said. "You gotta think about getting yourself a proper room somewhere."

"I'm not going back to *her*," sighed Terry. "I'd rather sleep rough."

Levi crossed to the tiny kitchen and lit the gas under the kettle. "I don't blame you, son."

"But, yeah, I know. I've got to find somewhere."

"And a proper job too," said Levi. "You don't wanna go working with scrap all your life. You're schooled. Not like me."

"Yeah."

"I suppose you've finished mucking around with this singing lark, have you?" asked Levi as he took out two mugs from the cupboard above his head.

"Yes."

"You was a fool there," added Levi. "The only traveller I know to be given a chance of getting out so easy and you go and muck it all up."

Terry snapped. "I didn't muck it up. I weighed it up, carefully. I decided what was the right thing to do. And I did it!"

Levi sneered. "Oh, the right thing, was it? You're given the chance of getting on the telly and making records and earning the sort of cash like none of us has ever seen before, and you chuck it all in and end up moving scrap metal for a living instead. And it was the right thing, was it? Right for who? Not for you, surely?"

"It was for my dad." Terry's voice was hushed. "It was for him. I told you. They were going to publish pictures of his funeral. Just to publicise a pop record."

"He'd have loved it," said Levi.

Terry was shocked at the comment.

"Loved it!" Levi repeated. "You didn't know him, did yer? You didn't know him like I did. You can't have done. He was one of the best, was your dad. *The* best. We grew up together, we did. Did the horse fairs. Epsom. All of 'em. I think I knew him better than you did. I knew him when he was well. When you and Billy was just chavvies. When his arms were brown and his face was pink. Before the ticker went. We did the hop fields and the fruit picking together… before it was all done in."

He spooned some tea into the pot and took a bottle of milk from the fridge.

"It was hard work. But he never stopped dreaming, did your dad. Was always gonna buy horses and show 'em at the fairs and that. That's what he wanted. Don't know where he thought the money was coming from." He laughed. "Yeah. Always dreaming, he was. Just like you. Chip off the old block, you are. He had dreams, just like you had. *His* never came true, God bless him. Yours nearly *did*. But you chucked it."

The kettle began to bellow steam. Levi didn't notice.

"Yeah, I bet he's up there now… in his white gown and his wings… and his new boots… looking down on you and saying, "Don't be an idiot *all* your life, Terry."

Terry shivered.

Levi smiled at him kindly. "Yeah, getting cold innit?"

Terry smiled back. "Kettle's boiling. You gonna make that tea, or what?"

Maureen wrote:

Dear Terry,

I've tried calling your mobile loads of times, but it's always switched off. That's why I've sent this letter. I thought if I wrote it all down, then perhaps you'd understand exactly what happened. Firstly, I'm so sorry. I wouldn't have hurt you for the world and to do what I did was really unforgivable. Having said that, I hope you can find it in your heart to forgive me.

Ray just turned up out of the blue, when I was feeling really low. I was missing you like mad because, what with you always going off to work with Levi, I hardly get a chance to see you nowadays. Anyway, he asked me to go out for a coffee with him and I had nothing else to do, so I went. I knew at the time it was stupid, but I was really fed up, just sitting in with Gran.

Well, one thing led to another, and he asked me out again. He's not like he used to be, Terry. He's not at all big-headed, and you think he would be, wouldn't you, now that he's famous? I suppose that was the thrill, really. Going out with a famous pop star. But I haven't fallen for him or anything like that, Terry. Honest. And when I saw you standing there in the doorway, with your holdall, I nearly died. I think Ray did too. If only we could have talked then, I'm sure we would have sorted it all out. I've been worried about you riding off like that. I hope you got back safely. Anyway, Ray realises how upset I am. And he understands that I won't be seeing him anymore. I won't, Terry. Honest. Please, please call me on my mobile. Or even better, come round. Please. Gran misses you too and she's furious with me. She said I was stupid. She's right. Please come home, Terry. I miss you.

Yours forever,

Maureen xxx

Terry read the letter over and over again. Then he tore it up and put it into Levi's waste bin, along with the rest of the garbage.

Twenty-four

It was just an idea and Terry was sure that nothing would come of it, but he couldn't lose anything by asking, could he?

He'd been thinking about it all day; sitting on Levi's settee and staring out at the churned-up mud and thinking. There was no way he could go on collecting scrap for the rest of his life, as he'd been doing for weeks now. He had to get a job in the business that he loved. The music business. Maybe not as a singer. But if someone gave him the chance to work in a recording studio, he could learn the trade from the bottom... and work his way up. In time, become a recording engineer, a producer even. If someone would only give him a chance. He'd run errands. Make tea. Anything, just so long as he was where it was all at. He thought about doing the rounds of all the recording studios in London. Just knocking on doors and asking.

Then he got to thinking about Scotty. He knew he had something to do with the production side of the business now that Bury The Rabbit had split. He'd read it somewhere. And he racked his brain trying to think of the name of Scotty's company. If he could find out where it was, he could apply for a job. Anything. He knew that Scotty hadn't been friendly when they were at school together, but he was sure it was only because of Rosetti. Scotty did everything that Rosetti did. But then, didn't everyone do what Rosetti did, even when it came to making fun of pikeys? Yes, Terry was sure that it was only Rosetti's influence that had made Scotty behave like that. But what was the name of the company he worked for? He just couldn't remember. But he remembered *something*. He remembered where Scotty used to live. His parents owned the large, white house on the other side of The Belling Estate. Not very far from Maureen's.

And he made up his mind. He'd go there. This evening. And he'd ask Scotty's parents for Scotty's address. And then he'd call on him and ask him for a job.

Levi came home to find a note from Terry saying that he'd gone to Berryfield's main house to take a shower.

The water felt good: warm and invigorating, his head tingling under needle-sharp jets as he altered the pressure control. He wondered if Scotty's parents would be at home. And he tried to work out what he'd say to them.

"Hello, I'm a friend of your son. Well, not a friend exactly. We knew each other at school. Terry. Perhaps he mentioned me? He didn't? Well, I'm the one that he used to bully. Along with his accomplice, Ray Rosetti. I'm the one who was put through hell, nearly every day of my school life, by Rosetti and your son. Terry Smith. Smithy the Gyppo. The thievin' pikey? Aah! Now you know who I am. Well, I was wondering if your son could give me a job..."

He laughed out loud as he rinsed away the last of the lather and turned off the shower.

"Whatever you do, don't tell anyone I'm here, will you, Levi?" Terry asked. He was worried that Joe Fisher might just turn up unannounced. "As far as anyone's concerned, you've no idea where I am. Right?"

Levi smiled. "Haven't clapped eyes on you for weeks."

"Thanks." Terry ran the comb through his hair and put on his coat. "I'm off then," he said. "I won't be late back. I'm going to see a man about a job."

There was no need to pass through Maureen's street. He could have taken the road parallel, to reach the other side of The Belling Estate. But it drew him like a magnet. He hoped in his heart of hearts that Maureen would be looking out of the window as he passed. She'd rush from the house and call after him and beg him to come back... and of course, he'd say yes.

Life without her was so painful; there wasn't a day when he didn't think about her, but he couldn't go to her. She would have to come to him. If she came to him… if she knocked on Levi's trailer and said, "I'm sorry, Terry. Can we get back together again?" he'd be so happy.

Levi opened the door and stared at her.
"Yes?"
"Hello, Levi," she said. "It's Maureen."
"I know who you are," he said coldly. "What do you want?"
"Can I see Terry?" she asked, nervously.
"No," replied Levi, remembering Terry's instructions. "I ain't seen Terry for weeks. And I've no idea where he is!"
He shut the door in her face.

Mrs Scott opened the door.
"I'm an old friend of your son…" he began.
She immediately called along the hall. "Phillip! It's someone for you!"
Terry was shocked. He wasn't expecting Scotty to be living there. He'd imagined he'd now be living in some smart apartment in London. He was even more surprised when Scotty greeted him like a long-lost friend.
"Hello, Smithy! He said, sounding really pleased to see him. "What are *you* doing here? Come in."
He led Terry through to the kitchen.
"We're better in here," he explained. "Mum and Dad are watching TV in the lounge." He switched on the kettle. "Coffee?"
"Please," replied Terry. He felt nervous. He was already taken aback at such a friendly welcome. Now… how did he ask for a job?

"Terry Smith? The fat man asked.
People rarely called on Levi, yet this evening he'd had three gorjas knocking on his door, asking the whereabouts of Terry. First there was that young Maureen… and now these two.
"Nope!" said Levi.

"Have you any idea where we could contact him?" Joe enquired.

"Nope!"

Joe looked at Del questioningly.

Del nodded.

Joe took out his wallet, opened it and slowly peeled off five ten-pound notes.

Levi shook his head.

Joe peeled off another five notes.

Levi put out his hand.

"Memory coming back to you, is it?" grinned Joe. He placed the money into Levi's palm.

"Wait there," said Levi.

He left the two men at the foot of the trailer steps and crossed the campsite to another trailer, which he entered without knocking.

A few minutes later he re-emerged, flanked by two tall, well-built travellers. All three of them strode aggressively towards Joe and Del.

"Oh!" gasped Del. "I think we've done it wrong, Joe."

Levi came right up to Joe and placed his hand heavily on the fat man's shoulder. "These are my two friends," he smiled. "Abi and his son, Jimmy. They've come to say thank you for the drink, gents."

"Very good of you," grinned Big Jimmy as he waved the wad of ten-pound notes in Joe's face.

"Good 'ealth to you," added Abi.

Levi whispered, menacingly, " Now disappear… before I set the dogs on you!"

Joe and Del left.

"I'd like to help, Smithy. Honest," said Scotty, "but it's really not up to me. It's Bif who takes care of the business side of things."

Terry's face showed disappointment.

"Look, I'll have a word with him," added Scotty, kindly. "Give me a call at KANSIT tomorrow." He handed Terry a card. "I'll be there all day."

And as he saw Terry to the door, Scotty was already making plans. He remembered when Terry Smith had sung at school. Hadn't he astounded everyone? Everyone, including Rosetti! That voice! Terry the Gyppo could sing. Really sing! And how Ray Rosetti hated him.

If Scotty could get Chas Atkins and Bif to listen to Smithy the Gyppo, singing… they might, just *might*, take him on. And think of the hype. 'Gypsy Boy Makes Good!' The old Rags to Riches story. It never failed. Yes, Scotty was sure they could do great things for Terry Smith. And Terry Smith could do great things for their new record label. And if they got him into the charts… how cool would that be? Oh *yes*! And if they got him to number one… yes, yes, yes! What would Rosetti do then, poor thing?

Twenty-five

Terry arrived at Earls Court underground station and walked to KANSIT, following Scotty's instructions. A crowd of girls lined the streets outside, sitting on the low, stone wall and on the bonnets of parked cars. Most of them wore T-shirts and badges bearing the name of their latest pop idol, Gary Brenn.

As Terry climbed the steps to KANSIT's reception, two of the waiting fans, both very young, rushed up to him.

"Are you going inside?" one of them asked.

"Yes," replied Terry.

"Can you get *me* in?" she begged.

Terry smiled. "Of course I can't," he replied.

Scotty had already told him about KANSIT's security; to give his name through the intercom at the main door and then wait until his identity had been thoroughly checked.

"Well, will you give him this letter?" asked the girl, pushing a crumpled piece of paper into Terry's hand. "Tell him I love him."

"Tell him we both love him," the other girl giggled.

"I might not see him," said Terry, kindly.

"Please!" the first girl pleaded.

Terry laughed. Had he not given up the chance of becoming a pop star, they might have been sending notes of undying love to *him*, instead of to Gary Brenn.

"I'll try," he said to the two excited fans.

He pressed the bell, gave his name through the intercom and waited for a security guard to open the door. As he entered, he looked at the grubby fan letter in his hand.

It was addressed to Ray Rosetti.

Terry took the lift to the top floor as instructed, hoping that he wouldn't bump into Rosetti. He wasn't sure how he'd react. He hadn't seen his arch enemy since that night at Gran's, when Rosetti had brought Maureen home in a taxi; the night that Terry felt he was capable of murder.

Chas Atkins and Bif couldn't have been nicer as Scotty introduced Terry to them. Immediately, Terry felt that this would be a good outfit to work for. He hoped they had something definite to offer him: tea boy… general dogsbody… anything.

"So what do you think of KANSIT?" asked Chas Atkins.

"I don't know," replied Terry. "I haven't seen much of it yet."

"We'll show you round later," Chas continued. "Lots of top stars working here today."

Terry nodded. "Yeah, I saw all those girls waiting for Gary Brenn."

Bif laughed. "They'll be waiting a long time. He cancelled his studio booking. He's doing *Chartbusters* today."

"There's someone else here who you might like to see, though," grinned Scotty.

"I know," mumbled Terry. "Ray Rosetti."

Chas Atkins was surprised. "Oh, so you know Rosetti, do you? Lovely lad, isn't he?" He grimaced.

Scotty laughed "Yes. Smithy knows him quite well."

"Shall we get down to business?" interrupted Bif.

"I notice you haven't got your guitar with you, Smithy," said Scotty, his eyes sparkling.

"Guitar?" asked Terry. "What for?"

"Scotty's been raving about your talent," explained Chas. "So before we offer you a job as an errand boy, we thought we'd give you a chance to audition.

"Audition?" Terry gasped.

"We'd like to see if Scotty's right," smiled Bif. "I'll go and get my guitar from my office," he added. "Why don't you two take the lad to the showcase studio."

Terry couldn't believe what he was hearing.

Rosetti was working with his producer, remixing a few of the tracks for his first album, simply entitled *ROSETTI*. If 'Down On Me Gently' were to reach number one, as expected, this album had to be ready for immediate distribution.

Franco had booked KANSIT's only available studio for that week; a cancellation due to Gary Brenn being offered an appearance on *Chartbusters*.

"Scotty's involved somehow with KANSIT," said Franco to his son, "so if it bothers you, we'll use Denson Sound Studios instead."

Rosetti smiled. "No. KANSIT's just fine, Dad. Couldn't be better in fact."

Rosetti was revelling in the fact that his solo single stood in the top forty and he hoped that he'd come face to face with Scotty. He couldn't wait to see the look of envy in Scotty's eyes.

Terry sang:

> "Gotta get myself in line.
> Find the words to say to you.
> Tell you how I feel, 'cause I'm
> Hung up, waitin' on you.
>
> Call on me,
> You'll find a stranger…"

Bif looked at Chas Atkins and grinned. Scotty was right. This boy did have talent. An extraordinary talent.

"Why don't you go and get yourself some tea, Terry?" suggested Bif. "Canteen's down in the basement. I want to have a chat with Chas and Scotty." He took his guitar from Terry and slipped some money into the boy's hand. "Order us *all* some tea and we'll join you in five minutes."

Terry left the showcase studio, almost in a trance. He hadn't been expecting this at all. He had no idea that he'd be asked to sing. And he was thrilled with the result. His voice had never sounded better. Maybe it was the adrenalin that had given it such power or maybe it was because, for the first time since he'd written the song, the lyrics had some relevance in his life. He could have been singing them for Maureen.

He pushed the button for the lift and waited, the song still going through his head. Bif had seemed delighted with his performance, and Chas Atkins had said, "So... a star is born!" Terry wondered if he was joking. Or did that mean that they were going to take him on? Were they going to give him a break? Was Terry Smith at last on the verge of becoming a pop singer? He tried not to get too excited. After all, he'd been here before, only to lose the lot. He wouldn't lose it this time, if it were offered. This time, he'd grab the opportunity with both hands. This time, it had to happen for him. There was so much at stake. He remembered young Billy's disappointment when he threw it all away the last time. And he thought of Maureen, who talked of the thrill she felt going out with Rosetti, just because he was a pop star. And most importantly, he thought about his dad and Levi's words, "He'd have loved it!"

The lift arrived. The doors opened. Terry stepped inside. The doors closed behind him. And there, standing beside him, was Ray Rosetti.

Rosetti was shocked. Terry wasn't. He'd been aware that this might happen as soon as he'd discovered that Rosetti was in the building.

"What are *you* doing here?" Rosetti snarled.

"An interview," replied Terry. He began to shake; a mixture of anger and fear. "An interview for a job."

"Not with Scotty?"

"Yes." He knew he should tell Rosetti to keep his nose out of it. It had nothing to do with him.

"What sort of job? You gonna be Scotty's Yes-man?"

Terry didn't reply. He looked up at the floor-indicator lights. Had he pressed BASEMENT? He couldn't remember.

"You'll do anything for a few pence, won't you, you pikeys?"

Terry told himself, Don't rise to it. Don't let him spoil this day.

"How's Maureen?" asked Rosetti, grinning widely. "Still seeing her are you? Or did she dump you after she'd been out with me?"

Terry silently fumed. His heart began to race. He felt the tightening in his stomach, the sickly feeling rising in his throat.

"Did she tell you how much fun we had, pikey?"

Terry turned to him. It was stupid. He knew he shouldn't have done it.

"You shut your mouth, Rosetti! Maureen's okay. *We're* okay. So you shut your mouth before I put my fist in it."

"Ooooh!" laughed Rosetti. "Temper, temper!"

Terry clenched his fists. He could feel his fingertips digging into the palms of his hands.

"I only asked about her because I care about her, Smithy. That's all," Rosetti went on. "But then I've always cared about Maureen. You know that."

"Shut it, Rosetti. I'm warning you!"

"She only went out with you because she felt sorry for you. That's all. She told me. She was always one for the underdog, was Maureen. And you can't get more underdog than you, can you, Smithy? Lowest of the low, aren't they, pikeys? Scum!"

Terry suddenly leapt at Rosetti and both boys tumbled to the floor, rolling over, punching and kicking.

The lift arrived at the basement and as the doors opened, they spilled out into the corridor, still thumping each other.

A group of musicians, just leaving the canteen, rushed along the corridor and tore the two boys apart.

"Come on! Cut it out, you two!" one yelled.

Terry stood, panting and glaring at Rosetti, his arms held behind his back by one of the musicians, a burly six-footer.

Terry looked none the worse for his battle.

Rosetti, still lying on the floor, mopped his split lip with a tissue. "I'll get you for this, pikey!" he said.

A security guard raced from the canteen. "What's all this about?" he asked.

"Dunno," smiled the six-footer as he let go of Terry's arms. "Think he must've heard Rosetti's new record."

Everyone laughed. Everyone but the two people concerned.

Rosetti got to his feet and silently made his way back to the lift.

Terry called after him. "Here. I've got something for you!" He followed Rosetti, took out the crumpled note from his pocket and handed it to him. "Love letter, I think. From two nine-year-olds!"

Rosetti snatched the letter.

"And by the way," said Terry. "I'm not here to be Scotty's Yesman!" He lowered his voice. He didn't want anyone else to hear what he was going to say. "I'm here to make a record."

The look of disbelief on Rosetti's face was something that Terry would never forget. Never! Even if he wasn't to be given the chance to get into the recording studio, it had still been worth saying, just to see that look!

Twenty-six

Rosetti sat in the rear of a limousine which had been hired to take him to the TV studios. 'Down On Me Gently' had climbed to number eighteen in the charts and today he was appearing on *Chartbusters*.

The swelling on his lip had almost disappeared. It was hardly noticeable now and, with a bit of help from the make-up artist, it would be difficult to tell he'd ever been in a brawl. He fumed: a brawl with Terry Smith! That pikey had got under his skin, yet again! But this time Rosetti had *really* got his own back. He thought about his schooldays and he remembered how Terry Smith had always made his flesh creep. Gyppos! Scroungers, all of them. Living off Social Security, paid for by the likes of his father. Hard-working businessmen like Franco, paying huge sums of money in tax, to support scum like Terry Smith and his family. And then Terry Smith had to go and top it all by stealing Maureen. She'd belonged to him and the pikey had stolen her... just like they steal *everything*. He'd taken Maureen away from him. And he'd never forgive him for that.

He'd enjoyed his recent nights out with her. They'd talked over old times and they'd laughed a lot. And things seemed to be going really well... until that time when they'd got back to Maureen's gran's and found Terry Smith standing in the hall, white-faced and shaking with rage. And when he'd gone, Maureen was so upset. That's what had really surprised him. She had the handsome pop star standing by her side and all she could think about was Terry the Gyppo riding off into the night. He couldn't understand it. How could she prefer that little nobody to him?

And now he was at KANSIT, making a record! For Scotty's record label. Or so he thought! Rosetti was sure he'd put a stop to that. Just one, short phone call. What that smug little pikey didn't know was that during his talks with Maureen, Rosetti had learned something about Terry's previous venture into the music business; how he'd made a record for Joe Fisher. And how he'd stolen stuff from Joe's office and disappeared. And Rosetti realised that Terry Smith must still be legally bound to Joe Fisher and that he had no right to go signing recording contracts with anyone else. He was still Joe Fisher's property. And Joe Fisher *had* to know! It was only fair. So Rosetti had found Joe's number and had made an appointment to see him.

Chas and Bif had put aside one of their own studios at KANSIT so that Terry could make his first record. Scotty and Chas had worked halfway through the night finishing the song, which had turned out well. Although it was still a little rough round the edges, a day in the studio would, they were sure, get them the big hit that they needed.

Terry was expected at noon. At ten o'clock there was a phone call from Joe Fisher. And all hell broke loose.

Terry took the tube to KANSIT, lost in dreams that perhaps this would be the last time he'd have to use public transport. Soon he'd have a hit record. Appear on *Chartbusters*. Sign autographs. The record company would get him a chauffeured car.

There were no young fans outside the studio today so obviously there was no one of importance inside. He pressed the bell and waited for the security guard to open the door. Bif was standing at the reception desk, waiting for him. And Terry knew immediately that something was wrong.

"We've had a call from Joe Fisher!" said Bif, sharply.

"Oh!" Terry responded.

Bif sat on one of the reception's sofas and opened his briefcase. Terry slumped beside him.

"Why didn't you tell us?" asked Bif, not looking at the boy. "Why didn't you say?"

Terry shrugged. "I thought it was all over."

Bif took out several sheets of paper. "This is the copy of the contract you signed with Joe. Biked over to us this morning from Joe's solicitor. We asked to see it because we just didn't believe it was true."

Terry looked down at his feet.

"We didn't *want* to believe it was true."

He handed the copy to Terry, who folded it in two and slid it into his pocket.

"Aren't you going to read it?" snapped Bif.

Terry shook his head. "What for? I know what it says."

Bif tried to remain calm. "How could you do this, Terry? You must've known it would come out sooner or later?"

"I didn't think he could do anything about it," replied Terry. "I thought he'd just drop me. He'd got nothing from me. No song. No nothing. And he can't force me to make another record if I don't want to."

"Don't be so naïve!" Bif's voice rose. "Of course he can! He can force you to fulfil your contractual obligations."

"He can't make me *sing*!" argued Terry.

"No. He can't make you sing," conceded Bif. "But then you can't sing for anyone else, either. Not for us. Not for anyone! Not even in a live performance. Ever! You signed a management contract too. Joe Fisher owns you, lock, stock and barrel!" Bif sighed. "What was your solicitor thinking about, allowing you to sign a contract like that?"

"I didn't have a solicitor," mumbled Terry. "I just signed it. I wanted to make a record."

Bif shook his head. He'd seen it happen to so many youngsters. Desperate to become pop stars, they'd signed away half their lives. Even *with* solicitors helping them, they'd managed to give away great chunks of their rights to record company executives. He also realised there was no other choice. Either sign on the dotted line, or be dropped for another bright young talent who *would* sign.

"So, what happens now?" asked Terry.

"Nothing," replied Bif. "Naturally we don't have any hold over you. So I suggest you go along with Joe Fisher's contract. You haven't any choice, have you?"

The phone rang and the receptionist picked it up.

"Good morning, KANSIT. Can I help you?" She paused. "Just a minute please." She called across to Bif. "There's a Mr Fisher to see you. Shall I pass him through security?"

Terry leapt to his feet. "Joe Fisher? Here?"

"You'd better talk to him, hadn't you, Terry?" Bif stated.

"No!" replied Terry. "No! No!"

Bif noted the fear in Terry's eyes. "All right, all right!" he said. "Calm down. I can't *make* you see him. Your future's got nothing to do with me, son. Not any longer."

The receptionist repeated, "Shall I pass Mr Fisher through security?"

"Yes," replied Bif. He turned to Terry. "Perhaps you'd better disappear to the Gents' for five minutes. I'll get Joe Fisher upstairs to the office. Then you can leave without seeing him."

"Thanks," said Terry. "And I'm… I'm really sorry about all the fuss I've caused. Honest."

He headed for the toilets.

"Terry!" Bif called after him.

Terry turned.

"It's a shame, son," he said. "A real shame!"

Twenty-seven

Levi pulled up outside the trailer, just as Terry was leaving.

"Where you goin'?" he asked.

"Nowhere. Just out for a walk."

"I wanna word," said Levi. He climbed down from his lorry, carrying a newspaper parcel under his arm. "Had your tea?"

"I'm not hungry."

"Got a nice bit of steak," he said. "Fell off the back of a butcher's van. There's enough for two."

"I'm not hungry," Terry repeated.

"Of course you are," he argued. "Get that frying pan going."

As Terry placed the cooked steak on the table... burnt... just as his dad used to eat it... he began to worry about 'the word' Levi wanted with him.

Levi shoved a large forkful of the shrivelled-up meat into his mouth, chewed, swallowed and then spoke.

"Now let's be having it," he said. "The truth, Terry. What about this singing lark?"

"I don't know what you're talking about," replied Terry.

"What about the record?"

"There isn't a record," said Terry. "I told you. I've given it all up."

Levi suddenly banged his knife on the table angrily.

Terry jumped.

"You liar!" he shouted. He glared across the table at Terry. "I don't mind thieves. You know where you are with thieves. But I can't stand liars!"

Terry was shocked at the outburst. "I'm not lying. There isn't any record."

"Liar!" Levi shouted again. "I heard it! This afternoon, on the radio! 'Terry Smith', they said. 'Call On Me'. Terry Smith. That's *you*, innit?"

*

"Gran!" Maureen called. "Gran!" She rushed into the front room with the radio. She was shaking. "Listen!" She turned up the volume. "Listen!"

Gran tapped her fingers on her jigsaw tray, hoping she was keeping in time with the music. She wasn't. But she wanted to display to Maureen that she wasn't completely past it.

"Nice, isn't it?" said Gran.

"Don't you recognise it?" Maureen asked. "Don't you recognise the song?"

Gran's face was blank.

"It's Terry, Gran."

"Terry?"

"*My* Terry! That's his song. 'Call On Me'. And that's him singing it."

"Never!" said Gran. "Turn it up a bit, Mo."

Maureen adjusted the volume.

"It is! Definitely," Maureen said. "I was there when he recorded it the first time, don't forget. It was the song he stole from Joe Fisher's office. He must've gone back to Joe and recorded it again."

"Well!" exclaimed Gran. "For rice cake! Why didn't he tell us?"

Terry had managed to convince Levi that he'd known nothing about the release of 'Call On Me'... that it was as much of a surprise to him as it was to Levi; that he'd thought the master recording had been destroyed.

Then they'd talked on and on into the early hours about Terry's career and what he should do about it.

Levi's answer was simple. "You go straight up to that Joe Fisher's office and say, 'Right! I'm here! So give me my share of the money, you thievin' gorja... or I'll do yer!'"

Terry had laughed at Levi's directness. But he wasn't sure if that was the way to handle the situation.

He laughed even more as he climbed up into Levi's lorry, wearing his ripped jeans and the working shirt with the buttons hanging off it.

"I'm a pop star," he said to Levi. "And here I am, shifting scrap metal."

They called, as usual, at the fitted-kitchen shop and as Levi negotiated payment for a couple of well-worn cookers, Terry picked up Levi's copy of *The Sun*. Aimlessly flicking through the pages he stopped suddenly at page seven... and he stared. He stared at the picture. He stared at the picture of himself! There he was, smiling at the camera and looking extremely handsome.

And the headline read:

'WHERE'S TERRY?'

"Levi!" he called. He jumped down from the lorry. "Levi! Look at this!"

Handsome, young Terry Smith may be bounding up the charts with his haunting ballad, 'Call On Me', but his manager, Joe Fisher, is hoping TERRY will call on HIM.

Schoolboy Terry made the record earlier this year and then... he DISAPPEARED.

Fisher, who also manages pop legend PETE SHANNON said: "Terry is very shy. When he realised he record was going to be a smash, he didn't think he could face the publicity."

So, where are you, Terry? Have any of you *Sun* readers seen him recently? If you have, we'd sure like to hear from you.

Terry read the article over and over again. There was no mention of his background. No mention of him being a gypsy.

"Bounding up the charts?" asked Levi. "What does that mean?" You got a hit record?"

"Sounds like it," replied Terry. "But there's one way to be sure."

Levi was as excited as Terry and could hardly wait to drive him to the nearest newsagent's, where they hurriedly flicked through copies of all the music weeklies, looking for a chart.

"This'll do," said Terry. "The Download Chart. It'll give us some idea."

Levi looked over Terry's shoulder as the boy ran his finger up the list of hit records. He found what he was looking for, closed the paper and placed it back on the shelf.

"Number twenty-seven," he said.

"Twenty-seven? Is that good?" asked Levi.

"Good?" Terry laughed. "Better than twenty-eight!"

Twenty-eight

'Down On Me Gently' had climbed to number six and Rosetti had been booked for his second solo *Chartbusters*.

"Dead important, this one, son," said Franco. "This is the one that could send it right to the top."

Rosetti climbed into the modified school uniform that he'd used on the video. It'd caused such a sensation among his thousands of fans, he had no intention of changing the image while he was on to a winner.

The assistant floor manager knocked on Rosetti's door, just as the *Chartbusters'* theme tune sounded through the dressing-room speaker.

"Stand by in the studio, please, Mr Rosetti," he said.

Rosetti headed for the studio, feeling much more confident than he'd ever felt on a *Chartbusters* appearance.

The audience applauded and cheered as the previous group brought their number to an end.

"Now..." the presenter announced "... if you've got a liking for school uniforms... then this one's for you. It's 'Down On Me Gently' from Rosetti."

There were loud screams from the audience. And Rosetti smouldered as he sang,

> "All I need is the opportunity
> to tell you what you really mean to me..."

The girls in the studio continued to scream. Rosetti peered through hooded eyelids, straight into the camera.

"… and if you feel you have to
put me down…
come down on me gently."

"Well done, son," said Franco as Rosetti left the stage to
thunderous cheers and headed towards the studio exit.

Rosetti stopped as soon as he heard the song. He knew it from
somewhere. He knew that voice. He looked up at the huge screen
suspended at the side of the stage; the screen that was showing the
video. A gypsy boy. Dressed in rags. Sitting at a camp fire. Singing,

"You call on me
When you are lonely
And I know I can only
Be a friend…"

And he realised that by contacting Joe Fisher, he'd started the ball
rolling for Terry Smith.

"Oh no!" he said. "Oh no! Please, no!"

"Cheers!" Joe clinked his glass of whiskey against Terry's glass
of coke.

"Cheers!" said Terry.

"I knew you'd come back."

"Did you? *I* didn't."

"Are you happy you did?" asked Joe.

"We'll see," Terry replied. "Depends what happens from here on
in, doesn't it?"

"Can only get better."

Terry smiled. "Or worse!"

Joe turned up the radio. Sunday afternoon… and the all
important pop charts. It was somewhere in the top five. They knew
that much.

It wasn't at five.

It wasn't at four…

"If we're not at number one this week…" said Franco Rosetti, "then…"

"We've got to be!" interrupted his son. "*Got* to be. If it's not mine… it's *his*!"

He paced the room like a caged animal. "I couldn't bear it if it was *his*." His hands were running with sweat. He wiped them down his jeans. "Please… let me be number one. I'll do anything!"

It wasn't at number three.

"And climbing to number two… it's 'Down On Me Gently' from Rosetti."

"No!" screamed Rosetti. "No! No! No!"

The police had cordoned off two of the main streets leading to the shopping mall as, after five weeks at number one, Terry Smith had been booked to open the new Megasounds store in the city centre. The girls had flocked there in their thousands, just to get a glimpse. Some had been queuing since dawn to get a closer look, knowing that if they bought a copy of the remixed CD, Terry Smith would autograph it. For some, that was almost too much to bear; to be that close.

"Just a few at a time!" called the manager as members of his staff opened the doors, allowing the first group of screaming fans to tumble inside. As each of them came face to face with their idol, most were reluctant to speak. None screamed once they were inside the building.

"Would you sign two copies for me please?" she said. "One's for my gran."

Terry felt his heart race. He looked up at her and smiled.

She returned his smile. She looked beautiful.

"You didn't queue, did you?" he asked. "Not with all these others?"

"How else do you think I got in?" she laughed.

The fans surrounding him, all eagerly thrusting forward their CDs to be autographed, now seemed an intrusion into his life.

"Terry… Terry… Terry…" They all wanted his attention.

"I'll call you," he said. "If you want me to."

"Call on me…" she sang "… when you are lonely…"

He smiled. "I *am* lonely."

"Then you know where I am," she said.

She kissed him on the cheek, then turned her back on him and walked away.

The doors were opened for her.

"Terry!" they screamed.

"Terry!"

"Terry!"

"Terry!"